Horns
of a
Dilemma

Horns

of a

Dilemma

Ganesh Krishnamurthy

PARTRIDGE
A Penguin Random House Company

To order additional copies of this book, contact
Partridge India
000 800 10062 62
orders.india@partridgepublishing.com

www.partridgepublishing.com/india

HORNS OF A DILEMMA
(A thinking man's cry from the heart)

Who am I; what am I doing here?
Life is confusing; endless, a sphere.
I get irate -- with people, with pelf,
Or am I annoyed with myself?
My Self? Who or what is it?
The Body? Or am I only a bit
Or, am I complete, the Whole?

Guide me, nay, Us. Give us Maturity
Objectivity, Understanding and Clarity
So we negotiate this life
Safely, and without strife.
I know not what lies beyond
This life, this large, murky pond.
Am I part or, am I the whole?

They told me early in school
Walk straight and narrow, like a mule
With blinkers. Neither left nor right.
So your life is full and bright.
But life is a dilemma whose horns
Cut me up, tear and dance
On the pieces. Am I still the whole?

***

PREFACE

This is a work of fiction. The origin of this novel lies on the Ayurvedic treatment table, with the therapist soaking my body in oil and pounding it with a collection of herbs wrapped in a leaf.

During the hour that I was on the table, the four different situations sprang up and the characters assumed a life of their own. These arose from my imagination and do not in any way reflect those of any real person and event.

When I got back, I scribbled down the thoughts and showed them to my friend, Shiv Nair. He read them and pronounced, "The four can be combined nicely to form a very good novel."

Thank you, Shiv, for that comment and the subsequent help in editing and polishing the manuscript.

As the manuscript began to take final shape, Sriram, my oldest friend, used his considerable skill in editing to fine tune it. Thank you.

When she started reading the manuscript, Deepa, my wonderful god-child said, "I genuinely wanted to know what happens next at each step. I think many people would enjoy reading this. Leave to me the task of ensuring that the world is aware of the book and has the opportunity to benefit by it." Thank you, Deepa. I owe you one.

Many peoples' lives have touched mine and sometimes gave me inspiration that formed the basis for some of the incidents in the book. Others helped by presenting ideas that I pounced upon and added to the narrative; yet others offered critical comments and thoughts. My humble thanks to all of them.

Enjoy!

CHAPTER I

It was obvious that she was in great pain. But the smile never left her face as she addressed her small audience. Vibhuti and Sridhar were sitting on the bed, Vibhuti holding Visalam's hand. Mark, Clara and Ali were sitting on stools and chairs, with Adrian and Ali's brother, Hassan standing behind them.

"It is almost time," Visalam said in a hoarse whisper, "I called you all because there is clearly a common destiny among you. You have–each one of you–gone through confusing times in your lives and have much to learn …"

Visalam broke into a bout of uncontrolled coughing, blood streaking the pillow,

"… from each other. Destiny has brought you all together here, from different parts of the world, with very different backgrounds for a purpose."

"*Perimma* (a term used to address mother's elder sister), relax," said Vibhuti, tears streaming down her cheeks. "We will all keep in touch with each other. Promise", she said, pinching her neck lightly.

"Life itself is a dilemma. At every step, we are faced with alternatives, many of them such that none of the

1

alternatives is without its own set of problems. Even though many of us do not recognize it, human beings inherently do not want to be hurt and, do not want to hurt another being. That is often the cause of our dilemma. However, we also fail to understand the not wanting to hurt another human being includes not wanting to hurt ourselves as well."

"Excuse me, Ma'm. Police Commissioner Rao has come to see you." said the nurse, peeping in.

"Please ask him to come in. I am almost done."

"Hullo, Visalam. I was in this part of town and wanted to come by and pay my respects. My wife and children also send their love and regards," said Commissioner Rao, taking his cap off. He was one of the many influencial people who had themselves been influenced by their contact with Visalam.

"Thank you, Commissioner; you have come just in time. My best wishes to you and the family" And then indicating the assembled people in the room, "These are very special people, who have converged here from different parts of the world. Vibhuti, Sridhar, you know the prayer for the well-being of all. Please chant with me."

Visalam closed her eyes and they chanted together, even as Commissioner Rao joined in.

> *sarve bhavantu sukhinaḥ*
> *sarve santu nirāmayāḥ*
> *sarve bhadrāṇi paśyantu*
> *mā kaścitdduḥkhabhāg bhavet*

As they watched, Visalam passed away with a beatific smile on her face. The evening sunlight that was pouring through the large window overlooking the garden seemed to dim a little, as if in salute.

Everyone in the hospice, other than the patients who were unable to move, came to pay their respects to Visalam. As the news spread, several people gathered in the hospice.

***

"I think there will a large crowd of people wanting to see her for the last time. She has been an inspiration to so many people. We need to make arrangements for parking, for movement of people etc. Let us use the hall as the viewing area, allowing people to come in through the east door and out through the north door. I think we should also provide lots of drinking water." said Susheela, the Trustee.

Lakshmi, Raghupathy the Administrative Head of the hospice, Radha, assistant to Raghu, Mariamma Kutty (still in tears) and another assistant were in Susheela's room, planning the various activities.

"Raghu, please call the Police Commissioner's office and ask for police *bandobast*. Radha, please take charge of the arrangements for viewing. Sekhar, will you take responsibility for all other activities--water stations, enquiry desks, and anything else you think we should have? I think the family has arranged for cremation at 4 pm.

Mrs Lakshmi, I understand you want to do the rituals here early in the morning. We will open for visitors to pay their respects to your sister by about 11 and keep it open till 3. The hearse will be ready by then."

"Thank you, Ma'm. We truly appreciate all your efforts and arrangements. Most of our near relatives will arrive sometime today or early tomorrow morning. Normally we would have taken the body to the house and then to the crematorium. However, we have told all our relatives that the body will go directly from here. I know this is not normal procedure here."

"Right. But then, Visalam was no ordinary person. Like all of you, I too believe she was a *mahatma*. We are doing something like this for the first time and I am concerned that all should go well. The plus point is that everyone is willing–in fact, wanting–to contribute, including the Police Commissioner. We have made arrangements for the body to be got ready and then kept in a casket with freezing facility."

The next day, rituals started early in the morning, with close relatives being present. The hearse came with a *pundit* and a woman to assist him. She seemed to know all the rituals and the preparations required. She had also brought all the things required–hemp rope, clay pot, etc. Interestingly, most of the people in the hospice wanted to be part of the rituals and followed the relatives, putting puffed rice in the mouth of the body. The entire ritual was conducted in the open area.

Vibhuti was inconsolable. She clung to her father, her mother and Sridhar in turns and was with her *perimma*'s body throughout. By 11, as promised, the body had been moved to the hall, and mourners started flocking in. Someone had thoughtfully put on some soft chanting of *slokas* in the hall. Although there was a large queue of people waiting to pay their last respects, extending beyond the gates of the hospice, the crowd was sombre and very orderly.

Several prominent persons, including a couple of famous actors, also came and were respectfully taken ahead of the queue by the staff or the relatives of Visalam. Some of the people wept; some sobbed, but most maintained a dignified silence. It was clear that Visalam meant something very personal and very special to many of the people who had come.

The body was taken to the hearse for transporting to the electric crematorium around 3 O'clock in the afternoon. Sridhar and Visalam's uncle went in the van, while the others followed in different cars.

Visalam's uncle had said that women were not expected to go the crematorium. However, Vibhuti insisted and travelled with Mark and Clara in one car.

As the vehicles left the hospice, the policemen on duty felt a sense of relief. Two of them decided to find a little shade, away from the eyes of the officers. They spoke in Telugu, their mother tongue.

"Whew, said one, what a relief. I did not like the idea of duty to guard a dead body. Who is she, do you know?"

"No. But I heard some people saying that she was a *mahatma* who had helped many, many people, including some ministers and film stars."

"Yes, I saw several politicians and some of the film stars. For this large a crowd, there was absolutely no untoward incident, no noise, no pushing and shoving. I was quite amazed that our own people could behave quite so well."

Another policeman joined them. "Someone was saying that her last few days were very painful, but she showed no pain. I see there are several foreigners here to pay their last respects as well."

A TV crew had set up its equipment nearby and the reporter and cameraman were focusing on the people milling about. As the cameraman focused on the anchor, he said, "Coming from a difficult background, Visalam lost her husband soon after marriage. She has since been a source of strength to many people, from the poor to the rich and well-to-do. The crowds are large and very mixed, with people from all walks of life. Let us get reactions from some of the people present here. (Addressing a young woman, possibly in her early thirties) Ma'm, how do you know of the Lady?"

"I know her only indirectly. All I can say is that she gave my friend a new lease of life. My regret is that before I could meet her, she was called to be with God", she said, with tears in her eyes.

An elderly man "I met her couple of times in the last few weeks. Being in her presence itself was refreshing and seemed to reduce tensions."

TV reporter. "I can see Mr. Reddy, the head of an industrial house and the President of the Chamber of Commerce. Mr. Reddy, what can you tell us about Lady Visalam?"

Mr. Reddy said with deep feeling, "She was an amazing person and her passing away is a great loss to all of us. I met her on the recommendation of my Director HR and was instantly taken by her *tejas*. She had extraordinary powers. In fact, we recommended to our employees to go and attend the informal *satsang* she used to conduct. Our HR reports that every one of the employees, who attended any of these sessions came back a better person, a better employee. The world could do with more people like her!"

Anchor, addressing another foreign looking gentleman, "Where are you from, Sir? How do you know of Lady Visalam?"

"I from Italy, and live in Hyderabad nearly one year. I meet her from the Rotary Club in Hyderabad. I can tell you she bring peace and calmness to people with any kind of emotional disturbance. She very powerful."

All of this was broadcast live, with soft *sarangi* music playing in the background.

At the crematorium, the body was laid on the floor while the priest chanted mantras. The priest then asked all present to walk around the body, starting with the family members. Later, Sridhar took a bath and went round the body three times still in his wet clothes and carrying an earthen pot with water in it. As he went round, an uncle made a hole in the pot to let the water out, signifying the soul leaving the body. Against protests by the priest and some elders in the gathering, Vibhuti insisted on being with Sridhar at all times.

The body was taken to the electric furnace and, along with the chanting of mantras, wheeled into it. In the final act, Sridhar was asked to press the button to start the fire.

Sridhar, Vibhuti, other relatives of Visalam, Mark, Clara, Adrian, Ali, his brother and a few others stayed on for a while. The priest told them that they should collect the ashes the next day in the morning and then go to a river near the city to immerse the ashes. There was a moment of calm silence.

Sridhar and Vibhuti agreed that their new friends could also accompany them in Sridhar's Mahindra Xylo, the vehicle carrying the ashes to the immersion the next day. Other close relatives were to follow in their own vehicles.

The following day Sridhar went back to the crematorium to collect the ashes. He was told to go the office, fill in the necessary forms and pay the fees. Sridhar was quite intrigued by the formalities required, but understood that it was necessary. The process took over an hour.

They all got into his car with the urn containing the ashes. There was not much conversation on the drive. Each seemed to be immersed in his or her thoughts. Sridhar drove expertly, avoiding potholes, cyclists and scooterists coming from unexpected directions. People in all varieties of vehicles seemed to love the sound of the horn. Sometimes the honking did not appear to be aimed at anyone in particular; just honking out of pleasure of hearing the sound or may be out of fear of some imagined danger. Sometimes the sound of the horn would lead one to expect a large four-wheeled vehicle only to see a youngster in a motorcycle whizzing past!

As they drove out of the main city, passing through Punjagatta and Ameerpet, they crossed several small hamlets. Adrian who had been fascinated by the contrasts he saw everywhere in India, would normally have been excited by the sights and sounds he saw on the way. However, even he was lost in thought.

They crossed the town of Buchapally and drove on to the river, where they were to immerse the ashes.

As they reached the river, they all got down, with Sridhar carrying the urn with the ashes. At the *ghat*, a *pujari* met them. There were several rounds of *dhaanam*, offerings made to various Gods as well as to the generations before. The money, of course, went to the *pujari* (and his team). It sometimes appeared that the pujari was interested in maximising the different types of offerings made to as many different groups as he could think of. However, the occasion being what it was, no one said anything but continued the rituals and continued to pay *dhaanam*. The pujari seemed quite at ease, as if he had practised these many times and knew how far he could push things.

After completing the last of the rituals at the bank, they hired a boat to go to the deeper part of the river and formally immersed the ashes in the water, along with the urn.

After the solemn event, they all trooped back to the vehicles in silence. One of the elders told all of them that they should wash their feet before entering their homes and take a bath immediately and soak the clothes they were wearing in a bucket of water.

As they were driving back, the mood was still sombre. After a while, Ali asked, "I heard people saying that women not allowed to go to crematorium, but Vibhuti go?"

"Yes," she said, "traditionally, women do not go to the crematorium. They usually stay back, wash and clean the entire house. Normally, no cooking is done in the house that day. Some friend or relative brings food for everyone, after the body is taken away from the house. I am not sure why there is this discrimination, but *perimma* was far too special for me and I wanted to be with her till the very end."

CHAPTER II

When Sridhar, Vibhuti and their new-found friends returned from the immersion trip, they decided to meet again later in the evening.

"I know of a nice, cosy little tea shop on MG Road. It is called just that – The Tea Shoppe. Say, around 6? Oh, yes, when you get back to your hotel, remember to take a ritual bath, wet all the clothes you are wearing now and send them for a wash."

Sridhar and Vibhuti arrived at the Tea Shoppe before anyone else. They claimed a table at the window and had extra chairs put in. It was a neat place, on the first floor, rectangular, with about 8 neat square tables, with comfortable chairs. One end of the room had an open, glass covered cookhouse, where a young girl was supervising the work of a couple of chefs.

The wall opposite the cookhouse was plain with a dash of bright orange colour, while the wall overlooking the street had large windows. Large photographs from different parts of the country covered the walls. Snow-clad mountains from the North, green forest dominated by a herd of elephants from the North-east, a group of ghumura dancers from the East, intricately carved lattice work windows from Gujarat in the West, a mud-fort from Rajasthan with camels in the foreground, unending expanse of beautiful beach with blue waters beating against the white sand from the Western shores of India, a Tanjore painting of baby Krishna and a statuesque brass goddess from the South covered these walls.

A young couple, whom Sridhar had met a few times, ran the Tea-Shoppe. The man, Keshav had quit his job as a successful salesman, saying he found the rat race meaningless and wanted to do something he enjoyed. He was also an enthusiastic photographer.

"Strictly speaking, as the closest relatives of Visalam, having participated in the cremation ritual, we should not be out like this. But, what the heck. I want to spend some time with these guys before they fly away to their own countries. May be we all knew each other in previous lives?" said Sridhar.

"I like this place. It is quiet and we get a lovely view of the street below. One could sit here sipping tea and enjoy life going by. Look, look Sridhar. Look at the old man carrying that big load. I was looking at him and thinking it is not fair that he should have to carry such a load at this age. Even as I was watching, a young man came up to him and offered to help. The old man haughtily refused!"

"You are making it up. How can you hear what they were saying from here?"

"Don't you dare!"

"Oh, there is Adrian, getting down from the taxi. And Mark and Clara. They are walking along, looking into each shop window."

"Hullo Sridhar, Hi Vibhuti."

"Hey. Look. There is Ali at the end of the street. I think he is searching for this place. Sridhar, please go down and bring him up."

As they settled down, Keshav came to the table. "Hi, Keshav", said Sridhar, "How are you? These are my friends from different parts of the world. I knew they would all love this place. Guys, this is Keshav. He is one of the few people I know who chucked a career in sales at a time when the whole world was beginning to open up to him to follow a dream. I know he now goes all over India cajoling grand old ladies to part with their secret recipes!"

"Thanks."

"Keshav, this is Adrian, from the States. He is one of those who will excel in any field."

"Glad to meet you", said Adrian as he stood up to shake hands, towering over the 5' 7" Keshav, "this is a really nice place you have here."

"This is Mark, from England. He has been in India before; knows a little bit of our country. And this beautiful young lady in the sari is Clara."

"Hullo", said Mark and Clara together, extending their hands.

"Hullo, very happy to meet you. Welcome to India and to The Tea Shoppe. Clara, you look very pretty in the sari. It is perhaps the most graceful dress for a woman, if worn well. You do full justice to the dress!"

"Thank you. This is a very tastefully done place" said Clara.

"Thank you. Hullo, Mark"

"This is Ali. And his brother Hassan. Ali came to India for a heart surgery."

"As*salaam aley kum*. Welcome. Hope your surgery was successful."

"*Wa Aleykumus salaam*. Yes. Very good hospital in Bangalore."

Keshav handed over menu cards to all of them.

"I will have your special masala chai. And your *sabudana chiwda*. Ali, try the masala chai. The others may find it a little strong."

"Oh, I would love a Darjeeling tea," exclaimed Clara, looking at the menu card, "And a samosa."

"Same for me, but no samosa", said Mark

"Ditto." Adrian added.

"Sridhar, Vibhuti, tell us something about today's rituals."

"Cremation marks the end of the physical body. The body returns to its constituent elements–space, air, fire, water, and earth. What we have done is the final completion of this part of the process.

All the rituals following this are designed to help what is left of the individual after the physical body is destroyed along in its journey to *lokas*, the other worlds. Our understanding is that no one ever dies, nor is anyone born. That sounds like a paradox. But what the Bhagawad Gita tells us is that it is only the physical body that is discarded."

"Right," said Mark, "Dust thou art to dust returnest. Every religion accepts that the body has to return to its constituent elements. The difference is, I think, in what each thinks actually happens to the 'person'."

"And how we allow the physical body to go back to the elements. Zoroastrians, for example allow the body to be eaten by the birds. In fact, even in our culture, *sadhus* are sometimes interred in a river after death to allow the fishes to feed on the body."

Adrian said, "Both of you chanted something with your aunt yesterday. What was it and what does is signify?"

"It is a very common prayer in many Indian households and in temples. It is meant for universal well-being. Literally, it means May everyone be happy, may everyone enjoy good health; may everyone enjoy prosperity and auspiciousness, may no one suffer."

Ali said, "I am Muslim. You are Christian, Hindu. But Lady Visalam not any religion. I think she even big from religion."

"I second that," said Adrian, "My meeting with her was quite a coincidence, but I think it was meant to be. I am now a lot clearer about how I should conduct my life than I was before."

Mark looked thoughtful and added, "I am really not sure what brings us so close to each one of you. I do have some Indian connection, through Clara. We have visited India several times and met some really interesting people. We have visited many of the temples in India, met men of great erudition, *sadhus*, as well as people who pretend to be something they are not just so they can get some benefit from tourists like us. But, no one like Visalam."

"How you meet Lady Visalam?" Ali.

"Hey, I love the title Ali has bestowed upon her. It suits her perfectly."

"It was actually a TV anchor who gave her the title. I agree with Mark it is apt. Why don't we share how we got to meet Visalam. Mark will you start?"

MARK

"That is a story in itself. Clara and I had been on a visit to the Sai Baba Ashram in Bangalore and were on our way back. We had checked in and were waiting in the airport, when all hell broke loose. Sirens screamed; armed police and army men everywhere. The tannoy came alive and informed everyone that the airport was closed till further notice for security reasons. No flights were allowed to take off or land. And no one was allowed into or out of the airport."

"What is tannoy?"

"It is a British expression for public address system. I think it derives from a company in Scotland called Tannoy that used to make PA systems."

Clara chirped in "I can tell you I was scared stiff, with visions of bullets flying around or a bomb going off. We were in the departure area, cut off from the arrival area. Everywhere I looked I could see men in uniforms carrying terrifying looking guns."

Mark added, "Fortunately, we were allowed to move around within the departure area. There were men wanting to get home, people needing to get to meetings, No one knew exactly what was happening, or how long we would be stranded there. Enquiries with the security personnel brought only one answer, "Please be calm. We are in full control of the situation. Everything will be cleared shortly." Airline personnel were also milling about, trying to calm the travellers.

Clara and I found some seats. People around us looked terrified. I suspect we would have presented the same look to the others. We were scared. Among the passengers, there were some who had started to argue loudly with the airline crew, but were told to be quiet by gun-wielding security personnel, who repeated the same answer to every query. Some started to pray, some started to cry and many were fumbling with their cell phones only to find that there was no signal. Looking back, as a group, we must have presented a weird picture – afraid, uncertain, furtively looking around. Right next to us was a pretty young Indian girl, who seemed to be unaffected by the chaos around us."

Clara said, "I first noticed her when she cajoled and calmed down a child whose mother was herself distraught. She stroked the child's head, and said some calming words, which seemed to work wonders. The child miraculously calmed down."

"Time stretched out with no information, no idea of what was going on, or when we could get out of this mess. Lots of rumours were floating around – terrorists have been trapped in one of the rooms; several people have been taken hostage; some drug or gun smugglers have been spotted; a plane has been hijacked on the runway, ... After about what seemed like eternity (but was possibly an hour or so), the airline staff gave us all some sandwiches and a soft drink. I turned to the girl next to us and asked, "Have you any idea what is going on?"

"No," she said, "but whatever it is, I am sure it will be resolved before too long."

Clara could not hold herself any longer and asked, "How do you manage to stay so calm when things around us are in such a state!"

The girl smiled, "It will pass, as must everything."

"You are amazing. Oh, I am Clara. This is Mark. We come from the UK."

"Nice to meet you. My name is Nimmi. This is my friend, Prakash."

"Do you live in Bangalore, or are you visiting?"

"My parents live here. I am on my way to Hyderabad."

After we finished the sandwiches, (still no wiser about what was going to happen), Prakash and I went to find a wastebasket to throw the empty plates and cups in.

"Your friend is amazing. She seems so calm and collected. Just talking to her has helped Clara and I become less agitated."

"Yes, she is very special. In fact, she lost her husband to cancer only a few days ago. The way she handled what would otherwise have been an earth-shattering event for anyone is amazing."

"What gives her this kind of strength? Has she always been like this?"

"No. I have known her for many years, but it is only in the last year or so that I have seen this side of her. We thought that her husband's illness and death had wrecked her internally, and it would all burst forth some time. She, however, credits her calmness to a remarkable lady in Hyderabad. In fact, we are on our way to meet her."

"Who is this lady?"

"She is called Visalam. A simple person, but with enormous power to help people around her find calmness and equanimity."

"Have you met her?"

"Yes. Her very presence seems to act as a calming influence on everyone. People come to her from far and wide, just to find peace within themselves – people facing difficult situations, confused people, ordinary folk,,,,, everyone."

"Whew. That sounds extraordinary. Is she some kind of guru?"

"That is an interesting question. No, she is just one of us. In fact, that is not true. We don't know much about her past life, but she is also a cancer patient, who has outlived all predictions so far. But clearly, she will not last long."

"Wow, if we have been taken so much by your friend's calmness in the midst of difficult conditions, her mentor, if I might call her that, should be truly admirable."

We returned to the seats. We were stuck in the airport for a long time. I must give credit to the airline staff. They too were under the same stress that all of us were under. But they showed concern for the passengers, remained polite, dealt with irate passengers fairly well, kept us supplied with food and drinks. We were fascinated by the stories Nimmi told us about Visalam. We found out that Visalam was in the hospice in Hyderabad and made up our mind to visit her. Nimmi gave us the address.

"To our eventual relief, things returned to some kind of normalcy after what appeared to be many hours. But being with Nimmi and Prakash, and talking about Visalam made the endless hours seem not so bad. We promised to look up Nimmi back in the UK, where she was planning to return in a couple of weeks.

That then is the story of how we came to know of Visalam and the extraordinary powers of this seemingly simple woman."

Sridhar said, "When I first met Visalam aunty, I knew there was something special about her. I really could not see what. She seemed to be one of the many simple people who have lived their lives in a small town with little or no exposure to big towns or cities. Vibhuti used to talk of her *perimma* incessantly - *Perimma* this, *Perimma* that. I got the feeling that here was a person who could do anything. And she loved her to distraction.

She visited Hyderabad frequently – of course, to be with Vibhuti! I got to see a lot of her and almost imperceptibly, I started to revere her. There was certainly something special about her."

"Aha, that was not your reaction the first time you met her," teased Vibhuti, "You thought her a poor relative from the village!"

"You, of course, raised my expectation so high; I thought I was going to meet God herself!"

"To me, she was no less than God. From the time I remember, I looked up to her for everything."

"I must admit, after the first few meetings, I too really looked up to her, even though we did not have much interaction. She was not as well-known at that time as she became later, and I believe she gained enormous internal power over the last few years," said Sridhar.

"To Vibhuti and me, she was more than special. What she did for Vibhuti – and for my sake – is perhaps the highest form of sacrifice."

"What did she do?" asked Clara.

"Yes, Vibhuti, tell us about it." Adrian.

"Well, she actually compromised on her very being, just because I asked for something that she could not afford. I was naïve enough to believe that she would be able to do it without effort. In fact, I thought she could do anything! I don't know. May be I wasn't even thinking about her, only about my own needs. But somehow, I had always looked up to her for everything, whether it was material needs or emotional support. It is only later that I learnt of the supreme sacrifice she had made."

The group was sensitive enough not to probe too deeply. They were lost in thought for a while.

"Ali, how did you get to meet Lady Visalam?"

ALI

"You know. One famous doctor in Bangalore say to me to go and see Lady Visalam. He said I must reduce my emotional stress and that medicine not do it. Medicine help, and exercise also help, and good food also help, he told me. For emotional support, he said I must meet this special lady."

"That's an interesting story. Tell us about it."

"I came to India, and Bangalore to get heart operation. Very good hospital, very fine doctors. In England and America they cheat. Too much money. Indian doctors very good, very kind and cost not much.

When doctors in my country tell me, I have to get heart operation, they said go to England. I asked my friends and all of them said England and America very, very costly. One friend tell me he recommend one hospital in India. I agree to come to India with my brother Hassan to meet doctor and am immediately impressed. Outside the hospital things not good, dirty. But inside, very good. The doctor explained very clearly and suggest operation. I said OK, and fix date for three weeks after. I went back home and then came to Bangalore some days before the operation.

The hospital room very good. Good bed, good TV, aircondition. Very clean and the nurses very kind and helping. Always there and ready to help. There is also one room for prayer, also for Muslim like me. Another for church, for everyone. Very good.

Dr. Hegde do operation. Very good doctor. He spend many time with me before operation and also after operation. Very friend and easy to talk. Afterwards I know he is world famous. But he talk to me like brother.

After successful operation, I stay in hospital for some days. My brother also stay in the room with me."

Dr. Hegde tell me, "You are fine, Ali. Your heart fine now. You must build strength. Three things important. Food; you must eat careful. Not much oil. Oil bad for heart. Eat small amount, but many times. Do not eat fried food. Avoid red meat. Eat lot of vegetable and fruits and whole wheat grains."

"No problem, doctor," I say.

"Two. Mild exercise. Go for a walk every day. 45 minutes."

"OK."

"Last. This is important. Try to reduce tension and stress as much as possible. Is there anything that might cause you stress?"

"No. But my son sometimes makes difficult."

My brother said," We will be honest to you, doctor. His only son, who grew up without mother, has been causing him a lot of stress."

The doctor smiled. "That sounds common enough. My own son sometimes makes life very difficult for me."

I tell, "You not only very good doctor, but like brother. My son Asghar has been a great emotional stress for me. I pretend everything OK, but I have big difficulty. I really don't know how to manage."

"Unfortunately, our medicine cannot solve this. But you must take care of yourself. It is important that you don't put too much stress on yourself."

"But how, doctor. What I do? I don't know."

"There is one lady in Hyderabad, who has helped a lot of people in situations like this. I have also met her. She is herself a cancer patient and has already outlived all predictions. She is currently in a hospice, really waiting for the end. I can tell you she is remarkable. If you want, I can put you in touch with people there. You can go and meet her. You have nothing to lose, but may gain much."

"I am already in position where I don't know what to do. I am ready to try anything. I get address from Dr. Hegde. He already telephoned someone there. After leaving hospital, I and Hassan go stay in hotel. Later, I and my brother go to visit the lady."

"What was your reaction to the first meeting?"

"We leave hotel about 4 O'clock in evening. It was raining very much. We take taxi from hotel to hospice. We are not sure what we find. My brother says he is Hindu lady and we should be careful. But I have seen India is strange country. I meet many Hindu, Muslim, Catholic, and the people with turban, what they call? Sikh, yes, sikh and have very good impression. On the way we see one church, one temple and a mosque very near to each other in busy area of town. Everyone doing their own business. Hassan was shocked. My doctor was Hindu and I have many respect for him. He is good man.

We reach hospice. It is nice garden, Clean, no noise. We go to reception and say we come to meet Lady Visalam. The reception lady tell us politely that she is under treatment and we want to wait? We say yes. She tell us we can visit the hospice, if we want.

"We wait for someone to take us. My brother ask me what is hospice. Dr. Hegde tell me that it is the last place for people with cancer who will die in few days. Hospice is not hospital, but also give medicine for pain. So everyone here is dying patient or with the patient.

One man came and took us on a tour of hospice. It was very good, clean and open. There was also room for everyone to pray – all religions. We also met one Muslim patient, called Jaffer. He tell us that Lady Visalam is wonderful person and can help anyone manage life very well.

We meet Lady Visalam near water lake. She is simple lady in Indian dress with big dot like many Indian women on the forehead. She smile at us and I at once feel relieved! First, we not talk about my emotion problem. Only general life. But I feel very good after that. After some time she go back to her room.

Jaffer tell me that they meet her in a group later in the evening. I and my brother meet some others in the hospice, go out for dinner and then come back to join the group for meeting. I saw also Adrian there."

"Yes," said Adrian, "I also remember seeing you there the first time."

"How did you come to be there, Adrian?" asked Mark.

ADRIAN

"Back home I am an active Rotarian for a number of years. Our club has done a few projects together with other clubs in Indonesia. But none in India. We have an interesting way of working in the Rotary. Any club can find a good project to do, and raise funds for it. They can then find a partner club anywhere in the world, who may be willing to put in an equal amount towards that project. Then Rotary International, from its own funds would contribute the same amount. That way, a club in the developing world can find three times the funds they can raise themselves for a good project.

Anyhow, I was in Hyderabad on a business trip and looked around for a Rotary Club to attend a meeting. This I normally do when I am travelling. I found one that meets on Sunday and called up the Secretary of the Club. As is normal, the Secretary warmly welcomed me to the meeting on Sunday. He also said that after a brief meeting, they were planning to visit a hospice where the Club was actively doing some work. They would be happy if I joined them for the visit. Again, it is normal for visiting Rotarians to be shown any project that the Club may be undertaking, if possible. I readily agreed.

In fact, I later found out that that Club was, in a sense, responsible for the hospice. They had raised the funds, got the land, got permission, got others interested in starting the hospice, and continue to support the hospice in many ways. The Secretary told me that some of the new members of the club had not seen the hospice and the work that the club had done there.

Come Sunday, I went to the Club and met some very good people. Once again, I have always found these visits to other Clubs outside the US very interesting and have met some really good people. I was talking to a few of them and the topic turned to the visit to the hospice."

"I was there last week," said one of the members and met Visalam. Amazing lady. Her radiance is simply amazing!"

"Yes, I heard she herself is suffering immense pain, but it is impossible to make out when one meets her. I am a keen observer of human behaviour. It is interesting to see how different people react so differently to pain. She is at one extreme. Pain does not seem to bother her much. There are others I know–including some in our own Club–who make such a song and dance about little pain," chipped in another.

"What struck me was her simplicity. Under normal conditions, if one were to meet her on the streets, one probably would not even notice her."

"She is simple alright. But hardly one of a crowd. I think she will stand out in any crowd of people."

"Right. What I meant was her simplicity. Her radiance does make her stand out."

One of them filled me in. "There is a cancer patient called Visalam at the hospice, who has been given only a few days to live. Yet, she seems to be a source of strength for everyone around her. So much so, that people from outside the hospice come there just to meet her and spend a little time in her presence. Her fame seems to be spreading very rapidly."

"I had already spent some time with the Project Director in the Club for the Hospice project and had taken the details for a possible joint project with our own Club. I was anyway rearing to go to the hospice. Now, my curiosity was fully pricked and I waited for the Club meeting to end so that we could go and see not only the hospice, but also this interesting person.

We drove to the hospice after the meeting. My first impression was very positive. That impression remained right through the visit. The place had a positive aura. You know, it is the kind of place that gives one the feeling, "God, I hope it never happens to me. But, should I come down with terminal cancer, this is the kind of place I would want to spend my last days."

We met one of the trustees, who took us around the very well maintained hospice. The people working there, nurses, doctors, cleaning staff all seemed to be acutely aware of the kind of work they were doing and I got the impression that they were doing it for the love of people who were suffering and for sharing their pain rather than as a chore or to earn a living.

As we came to the pool area, there was a small group sitting on the grass. Among them one lady stood out. Some people in the club meeting had described her as 'radiant'. I thought it was *mot juste.*"

"What is motjust?" asked Ali.

"It means the correct word for the situation. The word 'radiant' described her perfectly. She actually exuded radiance. I knew instantly that that had to be the famous lady, Visalam. There was nothing glamorous or otherwise outstanding about her. She was dressed in a simple white sari, with no ornaments or embellishments. Yet, there was brightness about her face that was unmistakable."

"That is Visalam," said one of the Rotary Club members who I had been talking to earlier. "Not all the people around her are from the hospice. Several are people from outside who come here just to meet her and find solace or, help remove some confusion in their lives. I have heard that many of them go away without ever talking about their problem and yet with a sense of peace within themselves. It is almost as if they don't even need to talk and get any guidance. Just be in her presence."

"I had myself been going through a difficult time in my own life and was in a bit of a dilemma. At the end of our visit, I told the Rotary Group that I would like to stay back and spend some time at the hospice; took leave of them and joined the group that was with Visalam. I noticed that the group was pretty mixed. There were Indians and a few white people. There was an African and, at least one Muslim. There were men and women of different ages.

One thing that was common among all the people-irrespective of their background, and whatever problem them may be facing. There was a general calmness. I am not sure what they had been discussing, but I felt that if anyone can help me resolve the issue that I was faced with, it was this lady."

***

CHAPTER III

After their evening together, each one wanted to know more about the others. No one had wanted the evening to end. It seemed almost as if they found in each other–with their common link to Visalam–an oar with which to row their life-boat to safety and sensibility.

"Can we talk more tomorrow also?" Ali had asked the previous evening. "This talk very good. I am very happy. I want to know more about Adrian ... Mark ... everyone. Now we very good friends, no?"

"I agree," said Mark and Sridhar in unison.

"I too would love to hear more about everyone. Adrian, isn't your flight tonight? Can you try and postpone it to tomorrow? It would indeed be nice to spend more time together and get to know more about each other," said Clara.

"Yes, my flight is tonight. I will try and see if I can get a flight out tomorrow night. I am not even sure they have a flight tomorrow. Let me check with the airline."

Adrian got through to the airline office, confirmed they did have a flight the next day, same time. Fortunately, seats were also available. However, he would have to go to the airline office in the morning and get the ticket endorsed.

The next day, Adrian and Sridhar met at Adrian's hotel lobby. Adrian had often wondered at this strange diversity in India–he had seen the very poor and the very rich; he had also seen dirt and squalor and the contrast in the hotel lobby that could compete with the best anywhere. The service in the hotel was impeccable, embarrassingly anticipating one's needs and ever with a solution-with-a-smile to any problem or query; in absolute contrast were the beggars and touts he had heard about (and seen a few). He had seen beauty in nature and in the elegantly sari-clad women in the hotel; he had also seen the ugly face of the country.

Adrian and Sridhar decided to walk down to the airline office. They spoke to the concierge at the hotel who immediately offered to get the endorsement done for them. "Great. Many thanks," said Adrian.

The plan was to meet in Mark and Clara's room at their hotel at 11.00. Sridhar said, "We have some time. Let me show you some places in Hyderabad that you may not see as a casual tourist."

Sridhar gave a parking stub to the *darban* at the main entrance to get his car. "Normally, I don't like to take the car—especially this type of big vehicle--to the part of the town we are going to. It is very crowded and extremely difficult to find parking. But today we will take the car, and then drive to meet the others."

"Where are we going?"

"Charminar. That itself is a tourist attraction. We will not go to the Minar itself. Instead, I will take you to some interesting side streets there."

After about an hour of interesting visit to the streets around Charminar, they picked up Vibhuti and started driving to Mark and Clara's hotel. Adrian said, "Wow! Thanks, Sridhar. That was a wonderful side trip. India is a fascinating country. I feel a certain richness in knowledge that is not available anywhere else. Yet there seem to be so many contradictions within. When I read that there is unity in diversity in India, I thought it was a clever turn of phrase. I am beginning to understand that the statement has far greater depth than is apparent. What we have seen today in different parts of this city is another reaffirmation of that statement."

"Even after being here for so long, I find the Charminar area fascinating."

"The Laad bazaar was something else. The colours, the sounds, wow. There are must be millions of glass bangles in that area! And the pearl market can drive any woman crazy!!"

Sridhar handed the keys to the valet, and they entered the cool, lofty lobby of the hotel. High ceilings, pretty, young girls--looking graceful in their traditional dress, the sari, soft music, people bustling about, feeling important. A few people were sitting in the sofas and chairs scattered about artistically. The central area had a large flower arrangement. A large waterfall added gurgling sounds of water, adding another dimension to the ambience.

"See what I mean about contrasts. Even within the city we saw marked contrasts. But compare this with

Laad Bazaar! I am not saying this is necessarily the better one – although I must admit, it is a lot more comfortable! Someone with an artistic bent of mind changes the central floral arrangement every day. And each is prettier than the previous. Awesome."

They entered the lift and went up to Mark's room.

"Hullo, where have you guys been?" said Mark, as they entered his room. Ali and his brother were already there.

"Hullo, everyone." Vibhuti

"We had some time on our hands and Sridhar has been showing me something of this great city that I would never have understood on my own."

"Sorry, we got a little late. We had to go and pick up Vibhuti also on the way back," said Sridhar.

"Fine. We have just ordered some tea for all of us. Shall I order some for you guys as well?"

'Would love a cuppa."

"Thanks."

"Where do we start? Adrian, why don't we start with what Ali was asking you last night?"

"Sure. About what my problem was. Right?"

"Yes."

"Something that I find many people facing, Ali. Certainly in our part of the world. You marry a girl with all good intentions, and then find that your needs, values etc. continuously diverging, allowing no possibility of a match. A few lucky couples find a convergence. Some find it running parallel and allow it to be so. But a lot of couples like me find the divergence increasingly growing the distance between the partners, making living together much more than a simple compromise.

Mind you, I am not saying one or the other of the two partners is necessarily right, or wrong. All I am saying is that the requirements of the two begin to open up such a wide chasm that there appears to be no way of bridging it."

Sridhar interjected "You can say that again. I too have observed this. It would appear that marriage is indeed a faulty institution. However, this is the only one that has endured the test of time, despite its shortcomings. In fact, I believe many societies, particularly the older ones, decided–for good or bad–that in a marriage, one of the two has to be subjugated to the other. In almost all cases, it happens to the woman!"

"Sadly true, with very few exceptions. There still are societies that are matriarchal. Even in India, there is a state called Kerala, where the woman still rules. She has right to inheritance, not the man," added Vibhuti.

"What this kind of divergence leads to is a situation that both suffer. Neither has a life that he or she would wish to have. In some cases, divorce is an option. But it is cumbersome, and often, financially crippling. People like me, brought up as we are in very conservative catholic environment, find it difficult to even consider a divorce."

"I make suggestion. Tell when you were child. Your parents, brothers, school... Want to really know," interjected Ali.

"I think that is a good idea. We have the day. And it would be super to know each other as well as we can in this time," Vibhuti added.

"OK. I was born and grew up in a medium sized mid-western US town. We come from a middle class family.

The main attraction in our town was a beautiful church. A river flows by the church quietly, and fishing was always a great past time for the residents. There were also historic walks, along wooded countryside. The town boasted a museum. Other than these, there was the town library and the cinema house that had been added later. There was not much in the form of entertainment, almost as if the citizens of this lovely town wanted no distractions from their prayers in the church."

Adrian was one of four brothers and two sisters. His father was a reasonably well-to-do lawyer. They lived in a large house just on the outskirts of the town. Among his brothers and sisters, Adrian was the quietest.

They were a regular churchgoing family. It was taken for granted that everyone would go to church every Sunday morning to attend prayers. On all major occasions too they would go to Church.

Adrian would listen to the sermons intently and was able to relate to most of them. However, he questioned many ideas. When he asked his parents, they often failed to give him convincing answers.

Once, when he was about seven, after a sermon about honesty, he asked his father "Do we have to tell the truth under all conditions?"

"Certainly. We must tell the truth at all times," said his father and told him the story of George Washington having cut the cherry tree and then telling the truth when confronted. Adrian had become pensive.

"Dad, when Aunt Caroline gave Mom the scarf on Christmas, she told her it was a beautiful scarf and that she would cherish it. That was not the truth. Because, later

I heard her saying she won't be seen dead in that thing. And I have never seen her wear it."

"May be she liked it at that time and then changed her liking?"

"If she really did not like it at all, should she have told Aunt Caroline that it was a horrible scarf?"

Adrian continued.

"There were some key incidents in my life that have created confusion or changed the course of my life. I suppose everyone has had such things happen to him."

"Of course," said Vibhuti and Sridhar in unison and burst out laughing. "Good luck," said both of them.

"What was that about?"

"Oh, we have a belief that when two people say something in unison spontaneously like happened just now, it brings good luck."

"Wow. My grandmother say something similar!" Ali exclaimed.

"It is amazing to see such commonalities surface across the world."

"Tell us something of these events, Adrian."

"When I was about 14 or 15, some groups of people were distributing leaflets telling us to become vegans. I was curious and read it quite carefully. Some of their arguments sounded interesting. They said that our dental structure was more like that of herbivorous animals, without canine teeth. They also talked about our internal systems–digestive systems etc.–which they said were not designed to process meat. I remember going home and examining my teeth to try and see if I looked more like a ferocious lion or a cow!

I actually turned vegan, giving up all meat and dairy products. My parents were very worried and I know they went and talked to the parish priest. However, it turned out to be one of those fads and did not last very long."

"But you are still a vegan," interjected Mark.

"No. I am now a vegetarian. Have been for some years."

"When and how did that happen?"

"In college, in Boston. We had a professor of Mathematics, called Prof. Srinivasan. Brilliant mathematician, great teacher, wonderful person. Some of us students would often gather in his office and talk not only mathematics, but everything under the sun. He told us that in traditional India, there was a culture of *ahimsa*. That meant that one does not kill another living being to feed oneself. In fact, *ahimsa* means not causing any kind of harm or hurt to any living being."

"In some cultures, eating halal meat has been accepted as common. We are used to it from childhood. Besides, even trees and plants are also considered living organisms."

"True. There is, however, a subtle difference. An animal is in a pitiable condition when being slaughtered. In fact, most slaughterhouses–even the modern ones that use many automated processes–do not allow areas where the actual killing takes place to be photographed or recorded. What turned me totally against meat eating is when I saw a film that actually showed the whole process. I don't know how they got permission to film it. But, when the animals are being taken to the slaughterhouse, they seem to know where they are being taken; there is clearly fear in their eyes and they cry piteously. The actual killing is gory. I am sure most people would find it difficult to eat meat after seeing the film."

Vibhuti chipped in, "I had a discussion with some of my friends on this issue and when I asked them why they stopped short of eating other animals such as horses or dogs, they really did not have an answer. They could only joke that they are more vegetarians than us because they only eat herbivorous animals!"

"That film turned me total vegetarian. In fact, till I visited India the first time, I did not realize how much variety there could be in vegetarian food! I spoke to my parents about what I had seen and heard. They talked about meat being natural food for humans and that the nourishment that one got from eating meat and fish were required for the body to grow normally. When I questioned them about hurting and killing other living beings for our food, they thought I was picking up strange ideas. I don't really blame them. They had grown up that way and had no other inputs to make them think differently. Also, I find that generally we tend to justify eating meat, but are unable to really come to terms with the concept of *ahimsa*.

I know that my parents were concerned that I was picking up these eccentric views. I know they discussed these with the parish priest, because he spoke to me once and when I explained why I wanted to turn vegetarian, he told my parents that it was a fad and would pass. It wasn't, and I continue to be a vegetarian even now. In fact, the more I think about it, the more convinced I am that meat eating leads to more violence in humans and in the world."

"I imagine your friends at school would have made fun of your habits!" said Mark

"What? With his size, I can't imagine anyone trying funny tricks with him!", said Sridhar, "A six-footer? And must be about 90 Kilos?"

"More or less. Yes, even in high school I was big and athletic. That, in fact, is clear proof against my parents' argument that meat was required for what they considered normal growth!"

"I know you played pretty serious level of basketball. Were you as good at sports back in high school as well?"

"Yes. My father was very proud of my achievements on the athletic field and in the basketball court. In fact, towards the end of my high school days, spotters approached me to try and get me to play professional basketball."

"Wow. With your good looks, build, achievements on the sports fields, girls would have been all over you? Were you also good at studies?" asked Vibhuti.

"Yes to both. Studies came quite easily to me, as did sports. I was pretty near top of the class in all years, both in high school and in graduate school. I did date a few girls, but was not especially interested in any particular girl. Coming from the kind of conservative background, I was also very careful that I never crossed the limit with any girl, even if she was willing."

"That would have driven the girls up the wall!" exclaimed Sridhar.

"Yes, it was a little awkward sometimes and some of the girls did spread stories either of my being a non-performer in bed or boasting about having seduced me into bed. Be that as it may, I moved on to one of the best schools in Boston, majoring in Developmental Economics.

I continued to play basketball and refused all advances to turn professional. That is not what I wanted to do."

Graduate school was quite tough. The competition was more than I had encountered back in high school and I had to put in a lot of effort to maintain my position in class. I did. Between classes, studies and basketball, I really had little time for anything else. I graduated pretty much close to the top of the class and was picked up by a very good firm in New York even before graduation."

"How did you find New York?"

"New York is a crazy place. Everything moves so fast, and if you blink, you can get cheated. It was quite different from the town I had grown up in, where things moved at a much more leisurely pace. I can also see why old-time New Yorkers love that place and will not trade it for any other."

"How did your parents take your leaving home to go to New York and to continue to stay there?"

"As I said before, they were proud of my achievements in school, but tried persuading me that it was better to go to the graduate school near home, rather than go to Boston. However, I preferred to go the Boston. They were not happy about it. The only time they came there was for my graduation ceremony and that after a lot of persuasion. They did not like New York one bit!

I did not make many close friends. I found most New Yorkers too slick. I did have several friends, but very few I could call close. It was under these conditions that I met Rose."

"Your wife-to-be?"

"Yes. Rose was a beautiful girl, from a town similar to my own. She was bubbly, vivacious and had come to New

York looking for excitement. Something more than she found in her own home town."

ROSE

She couldn't wait to finish high school and get out of the dreary town. Rose had heard so much about New York. That, she felt, was what life was really all about. The life her parents were living was drudgery, even if they did not recognize it.

Rose was 5' 5", beautifully sculpted, with a skin that was translucent, without any blemish. She was prom queen at high school whom every boy worth his salt wanted to date. Rose was haughty, and picky about whom she dated. On finishing school, she took whatever money she had, borrowed some more from her parents and set out to New York.

New York was everything she had dreamt of. Yet, she found New York and New Yorkers frightening, despite her ambitions to make it big. Rose got a job as an assistant to a Manager in an accounting firm. She knew her only asset was her beauty and was determined to use it to full advantage. She seriously dated two business executives, but both came to nothing.

The first time she met Adrian, she was immediately attracted. When she found that he was one of the rising stars in his company, she spent as much time as she could with him. Despite her hankering for a life on the fast lane, she found something calming about him.

"It is a good thing, girl," she told herself, "push it along." There was, however, a portion of her that said she could do better, even if it meant looking for a slightly older man, ideally from a rich family background.

Rose found the evenings spent with Adrian relaxing and happy. She was offended when he politely let pass every signal she sent that she would be happy to go to bed with him. One evening, back in her apartment, she looked at herself in the mirror closely, inch by inch. "Shiny blond hair, facial features any Hollywood star would be proud of, soft, rounded lips that many would pay to kiss, firm breasts, figure of a leading model, ...Heck, I AM beautiful. What is holding Adrian back?"

They spent many evenings together outside–at a theatre, a cinema, or a good dinner, but rarely at his or her home. They touched each other at every opportunity, indulged in heavy petting, but never had intercourse.

Rose had a two-week vacation coming and decided to go visit her mother, who had been unwell for some time. That weekend Adrian went out on a double date with a colleague from the office. She was smart, chic and a very good conversationalist. They had a wonderful evening, with Adrian dropping his date back at her apartment and leaving her with a goodnight kiss.

On the following Friday he went for a movie again with the same girl, followed by dinner. Once again, Adrian dropped her back and drove off after a longer goodnight kiss.

On Saturday, she was going to travel to Singapore on vacation. He offered to drive her to the airport and see her off. They had lunch together and then drove to the airport. He was extremely happy during this period.

On her return, he told Rose about the dates, and she flew into a rage, something he did not anticipate and it shook him. "As soon as my back is turned, you go on a series of dates, smooching around with some girl! I never want to see you again." She stormed off and was very moody over the next few days.

"How dare he go around with that bitch!" she thought to herself, "trying to steal him from me the moment my back is turned. I have to find a way of locking him in."

When they met the next time, Adrian tried to explain that it was only a harmless date, one of them with other friends. He hinted that Rose and he were neither engaged nor married for her to get so upset about his seeing a girl a couple of times. She would not be mollified. Over the next few days he paid her great attention and they resumed their evening outings.

One Saturday evening Rose offered to cook dinner at home. They rented a wonderful old film, starring Richard Burton and Elizabeth Taylor. They had a great evening, although the dinner itself was nothing to write home about. Adrian had brought a scrumptious cake for dessert. They lounged around in the couch, watching the movie and gently petting. As soon as the movie was over, Adrian got up and said he had to travel out of town early the next morning and had to get back. With a peck on her cheek, he got into the car and drove off.

"I can't stand this much longer," screamed Rose, as soon as she closed the door. The plate she threw crashed on the door with a loud noise, followed by a couple of cups. "This is really stupid. I am going to kill him." She poured herself a strong drink and crashed into the couch.

Life drifted along on similar lines for the next several weeks. Adrian was quite busy at work, but would generally take Rose out for a movie or an outing over the weekend. He wasn't sure where this was leading.

Some weeks later, one Monday, he had to travel out of town on work and was away for most part of the week. On Thursday, he got a call from Rose.

"I am scared, Adrian. Please come back," she cried, "I have never seen death at such close quarters."

"What happened? Were you in an accident? Are you OK?"

"I am scared, scared" she sobbed.

After she had calmed down a bit, she told him that her boss had died in office. He had called her into his office for some discussions. One minute he was leaning back in his chair, talking to her and the next minute he had crashed to the floor with a cry. He twitched a couple of times and then went quiet. She was stunned for a minute and then ran screaming across the hall. By the time the ambulance came, she was sure he was dead. Rose was pale and started shivering. She also was rushed to the hospital. At the hospital, he was pronounced DOA, Dead on Arrival. Rose was given some attention in the emergency room and discharged. She was allowed to go home. However, she had not got over the entire event. As soon as she got home, she had called Adrian.

On his return two days later, Adrian went straight to see Rose. She clung to him and wouldn't let go. "Adrian, I have never been so scared in my life. I don't want to die. I don't want to be alone. Why did you have to go away now? I had to go and sleep in my friend's house last night."

Rose was genuinely frightened. She had never thought about death. In fact, her boss was a good-looking man, and Rose had had an eye for him. She just could not reconcile with his death; with death that she saw at such close quarters.

Her first reaction was, "Oh, My God. I don't want to die! This is weird. I don't want to die."

ADRIAN

"When I got the call from Rose, I was actually in the middle of some work. She sounded so frightened and lost that I did not know what to tell her except to say everything will be fine. And that I would come as soon as possible.

I was not really able to focus on my work till I finally took the flight back to New York. During this period, I spoke to Rose several times. Although she slowly gained more control over herself, she was still near hysterical every time we spoke.

"I am ready to board the flight. I will come directly to your apartment," he told her on the last call from the airport.

"I went from the airport directly to her place. She had been given the next day off from work, after her reaction and some attention at the hospital. As soon as I entered her apartment, she flung herself on me and started to sob uncontrollably. I held her close and reassured her that everything would be fine, now that I was there to take care of her."

"Adrian, it was horrible," she continued to sob, "Stephen just dropped off the chair, even as he was talking to me. At first I thought the castors on the chairs had slipped. But something told me that it was worse, far worse. I have never seen a dead body before. He was alive just a moment before and suddenly.... I did not know what to think or do. I just screamed and ran out of his office."

"Relax, Sweetheart. Everything will be just fine."

"Please don't leave me and go anywhere. I am scared to be alone."

Adrian continued. "My thoughts were zigzagging. Here I was, hugging a beautiful girl, comforting her, providing her support, protecting her from the big, bad world and her worst fears. I went through a welter of emotions–sympathy, protectiveness, honour, desire–all clashing with one another. I continued to hold her for a long time, till she calmed down and then sat her on the couch."

"Rose, let's get married."

Her face lit up. Rose could not believe it! Adrian was proposing to her!!! All her fears vanished almost as if blown away by a gentle breeze. They were sitting on the couch. She looked at him and stared into his eyes–full of love and sympathy. She did not say anything, but slowly moved her face close to his and closed her eyes. He kissed her, gently at first, and then with the full force of pent up passion. Adrian lost all control; great urgency was bursting in both of them as they tore off their clothes. Before long, she was on the couch, the carnal energy that Adrian had been denying himself burst forth like a dam that had given way. Finally, he flopped on top of her, supporting his weight on his hands and knees.

Adrian felt complete, as he snuggled with Rose on the couch. "That was amazing," he said, "You are the most beautiful person the whole world. Hey, do I take it as Yes?"

"Yes, yes, yes. I want to be your wife."

They washed up and went out for dinner. He was considerate as always, but she was amused to see that he looked a little bit nervous! After a wonderful dinner, they walked on the streets for quite some time, holding hands, suddenly stopping to kiss. When they returned to her apartment, she insisted that he stay overnight. "You have all your things with you. Stay the week-end with me."

She showered before Adrian went in for a shower. Waiting for him in bed, she was still pretty excited. When he came into bed, she whispered, "I already feel we are married."

They made slow, ecstatic love, lasting well into the night and fell asleep in each other's arms. Unlike the men she had known before, he did not just turn the other side and go to sleep.

ADRIAN

"That was quite an evening. I had maintained strictly that sex should be only between married partners. I know it sounds old-fashioned, but that is how I was brought up and that is how I felt. The whole evening and night is just a blur. There were too many emotions jostling for space in my mind, pushing at each other. I wasn't sure whether I was doing the right thing–both in terms of going to bed with her and indeed, whether we were really suited for each other. But there was a sense of *noblesse-oblige* and there was no rethinking. I was determined to do whatever it takes to make our lives enjoyable for both of us.

Next Friday we flew to my hometown to meet my parents. I did not expect it to be a great get-together. It wasn't. It was worse; really forgettable. My parents, especially my mother, seemed to think Rose was totally unsuitable for me. While she was polite to Rose, both my parents tried to persuade me that I was making a bad choice. Rose, on her part, did nothing to make things easier. She clearly looked down on my folks, thought they were unsophisticated. Although she did not do or say anything that would break the whole thing, her attitude was clearly not to my parents'–or for that matter my siblings'–liking. However, I pressed along. I had made a commitment, and could not very well back out. I just hoped and prayed that things would work out.

We returned to New York and settled down to the pattern of life. Those days my work took me out of New York quite often. We spent as much time together as possible when I was in town. We also flew down to meet her parents one week-end. While it was better than the visit to my parents, I did find her family very different from how I had grown up. Church did not seem so important to them and I did find her sister a little odd. I had a colleague at work in New York who was from the same town as Rose's parents. He seemed to know the family but refused to talk about them. On my pressing him, he said Rose was perhaps OK, but some others in the family were a bit off-centre. He wouldn't say anything further.

During the engagement period, I often found her moody. She was also very demanding. She quizzed me about my work, who my boss was and what my prospects of my career growth were etc. She tried telling me that I ought to be more demanding at work, and aggressively pursue my salary increases and promotions.

We were married later that year at a small church in Rose's parents' place. It was a quiet wedding. Following the wedding, we had a couple of good years, and in time, had a son, Paul. I enjoyed the years when he was growing up.

I wanted to get Paul to church regularly, but Rose always seemed to have other plans. I was perhaps too soft and did not press. Unfortunately for all of us, including Paul, the differences between Rose and I kept widening. She was ambitious and wanted to get to the top of the social ladder. She kept pressing me to be more demanding at work with clear goals for promotion. She chose who our friends would be, and discarded, one by one, most of my old friends. The new friends we moved with were chosen by Rose based on how that would affect her move upwards. She liked to throw fancy parties and ensure that the people who may help us be seen to be among the social elites were invited.

Looking back, I feel maybe I could have been more assertive and put my foot down on many things that we were doing that I felt were either unnecessary or sometimes even incorrect. If I had done that, I am not sure what the outcome would have been; what would have happened to our marriage. However, I did not, and allowed things to happen. I remember an incident when she wanted to watch soap on the TV in our bedroom, while I wanted to sleep. I was tired after a difficult day at work and really wanted to sleep. I asked her to switch the TV off, or at least reduce the volume to a very low level. She would do neither. I picked a pillow and a sheet and went to the guest room. After a few minutes she came and persuaded me to return to the bedroom, but continued to watch the programme exactly the way she was watching earlier. That is how assertive I was! In fact, I realized later, she had waited for a commercial break to come and persuade me to return to our bedroom.

Fortunately, my professional life was on the up. I was successful and the firm recognized my contributions. I rose quickly in the hierarchy. In view of what was happening at home, I concentrated on doing my best at work. Work also took me out of town frequently and sometimes out of the country. On a couple of trips to Europe, Rose also joined me. Europe fascinated her and she started to fill the house with things from Paris, Milan and London.

After my promotion to Head of Division, Rose insisted we move to a bigger apartment in a more upmarket area in town. I did not argue with her, though I felt that the place we had was just fine. It was convenient for everything including Paul's school. However, Rose wanted to move him to a new school as well.

I wanted my parents to come and live with us in New York, but they refused to move out. They said they were happy there, and if we wanted to meet them, we could come down. That did not happen very often. Rose did not want to go there, nor did she want Paul to spend too much time there. She always had alternate plans for our vacations and, had her way. It is not as if these were unhappy vacations. We went to some real wonderful places and all three of us did enjoy ourselves."

"Did Paul also turn vegetarian, like you?"

"No. In fact, Rose would ridicule my idea of being a vegetarian and make fun of me in front of him. She encouraged him to try all types of food. I tried telling him why I was a vegetarian and that he should take his own decision about such things when he grew up. Somewhat naïve, perhaps."

"You seem to have had rather a difficult life. But you are rather soft, you know," said Vibhuti, "A gentle giant. It is sad to hear your story. I am sure Rose was not the ideal girl you imagined you wanted to spend your life with."

"Right. Now that we are talking freely, I will also tell you that there were times I would think back on my life before marriage and wish I could go back. Driving back from work one day, I realized that I was not looking forward to it. The only attraction I had at home was Paul. I started to imagine the qualities I would love in the woman of my dreams. Rose was a far cry from it."

"Couldn't you have got a divorce?"

"Yes, I could. For one, the idea of divorce was not really something that appealed to me. Two, I wasn't sure that was the best way forward, especially for Paul. I was also pretty certain that Rose would contest it bitterly. Not because staying married is what she wanted, but I sensed that she could be pretty vindictive. I was not willing to face that. However, thoughts of being with another girl, more suited to my own personality and temperament did keep popping up.

It was around this time I met Julia. It was at JFK on one of my trips out of town on work. I was in the book store browsing, when I saw her. "Julia, of all people. What a pleasant surprise!"

Julia was some years my junior at high school. Her brother Jack and I were in the athletics track team. I had met her several times in school. She was a pleasant, warm, bright girl.

"What brings you to New York. Have you moved here?"

"Yes, I moved a few months ago. Jack had told me you were in New York, but did not know your whereabouts."

"I got talking to her and found that she had finished high school and then married a teacher at the local school. However, he had turned out to be good-for-nothing and was thrown out of school after he had been caught making advances to some of the students, although he declared to everyone that he had quit work to devote his time fully to writing a novel. He had no work, except an occasional piece he managed to write for the local paper. Meanwhile, Julia had held down a job and managed to get a diploma in personnel management. Her husband had taken to drinking and continued to chase other women. It wasn't long before the marriage turned sour and ended in a divorce. Fortunately, there were no children. Julia had felt stifled in her hometown and, with her added qualification, found a job in New York.

I was sad to hear her story. She had been so full of life, always eager to learn new things, generally happy under most situations. She seemed to have taken the divorce well, and had decided to go on with her life. We parted when my flight was announced, after exchanging contact details.

When I returned to New York, I told Rose about the chance meeting with Julia. She showed no interest, being preoccupied with selecting a dress for a formal dinner we had been invited to.

A few days later I called Julia. Her office was not far from mine in Manhattan and we decided to meet for lunch. Though brief, it was really nice to spend time with her, catching up on all the gossip from back home.

The following week Rose was throwing a party at home and I invited Julia. Rose wasn't particularly happy, saying she would not fit into the crowd. However, I had already invited Julia and I let it be. Unfortunately, Julia was out of place among the people Rose had invited. Rose pointedly ignored her. Although Julia was pleasant to everyone, including Rose, she told me later that she was quite uncomfortable.

I invited Julia home for dinner a couple of times. Rose, however, continued to be cold to her, and sadly, Paul took the cue from his mother. I stopped calling her home, but continued to meet her regularly. We met mostly for lunch. We were very comfortable with each other and enjoyed these outings very much. Our relationship was purely platonic. I did mention to Rose about our meetings at lunch off and on, but she did not seem interested.

On one such occasion at lunch I told Julia that I had to go to Chicago for a couple of days the following week on work. Julia's face lit up as if a thousand watt bulb had been switched on."

"Wow. This is unbelievable. And wonderful. Only a couple of days back, I have been asked to go to our Chicago office. I am supposed to fix up the date with them. Incredible. Let's go together. I will confirm it by tomorrow."

"Julia's excitement was infectious. I was very happy and felt that it would be real nice to travel with her. Travel for me is usually drudgery. I take some work with me and spend much of my time at the airport and in flight completing work. This promised to be a much more pleasant journey. I told her which hotel I generally stay in and she said she would book herself in the same hotel.

I have heard say that time is not absolute. I can vouch for it. Normally, these flights would feel like they go on for ever. This trip, however, the wait at the airport and the two-and-a-half hour flight seemed to vanish in a jiffy. It seemed as if we had been talking only for a few minutes when the pilot announced descent into O'Hare. We took a taxi to the hotel together."

CHICAGO

The first day in Chicago was crazy, and Adrian returned to his room rather late, after having a working dinner with his colleagues. He had called Julia and told her about it. The next day, fortunately, was not so heavy. After the day's work, Adrian took Julia out to dinner. Even as they were having dinner, both could feel a storm building up. Their conversation seemed to stop every once in a while, even as it was flowing easily. Unspoken, unsaid words and meanings seemed to zip back and forth like two-way lightning. Their eyes clashed across the table, producing unseen energy and leaving both of them speechless. Adrian put his hand on hers–lightning that was flashing across the space between them suddenly seemed to have found a conductor. Julia pulled her hand away as if struck by a bolt. Her cheeks looked the colour of ripe tomatoes, as she avoided Adrian's eyes in shyness that she had never before experienced.

After dinner they walked back to the hotel and Adrian walked across to see her at her door. Both bodies seemed to be charged with static electricity that was so strong that it is wonder it did not create any disturbance in the electrical equipment along the street and in the corridors. They stood at Julia's room door for several minutes – Adrian searching Julia's eyes and hers locking into his one moment and shying away the next. Finally, Adrian slowly pulled her to him and kissed her gently. She completely melted into him fusing as if they were one body, not two. As the kiss lingered, Julia responded to kiss. They finally broke the kiss, pulled apart and both almost simultaneously said, "We shouldn't!"

Adrian quickly walked back to his room, thinking about what happened. His mind was a whirl. He could feel the inevitable pull towards Julia. He had never thought of having an affair, but Julia fitted his own description of the girl he would like in his life like a high precision engineering component. He realized how much she meant to him. He just could not stop thinking about her.

His hotel phone rang. "Adrian....." said Julia.

"Don't say another word, Julia. I am coming over."

Adrian went to Julia's room, locked the door and put on the DND sign. He looked at her. "Everything a woman should be," he thought to himself, as she once again dissolved in his arms. "Oh, Adrian," she mumbled as she hid her face in his chest.

Adrian lifted her chin, and stared into her fathomless deep eyes. He bent down and kissed her tenderly. He kissed her eyes, her forehead, her cheeks, her lips.

They made love through the night, wondering at the amazing feelings that each generated in the other. Adrian knew Julia was not the most beautiful girl in the world, but in his mind she was everything that he had ever imagined a perfect woman should be.

JULIA

When Julia first arrived in New York, she was very wary. She had been warned about the big bad apple and how a girl from a small town could easily be taken advantage of. She looked at everything in wonder. People seemed to be jostling each other for space and appeared to be headed somewhere in a hurry. Julia was had come to New York to try to erase the bad taste that her bad marriage and divorce had left in her.

She joined work, found a Studio apartment and began a life with the sole intention of forgetting the bad experiences she had gone through.

Work was interesting and she found her colleagues very nice. She made a few good friends, but generally spent her time with her music and going to concerts. Over time, she did develop a small circle of friends who were also interested in music. She would sometimes spend an evening with one or more them either going to a concert or trying their hand at some music in one of the homes.

Julia had come to New York to try and forget her rather bad marital experiences in her home town, but could not really come to terms with either her situation or with New York. She longed for some of the things she missed from home and kept hoping she could meet someone from home.

Running into Adrian was almost as if her unsaid prayer had been answered. She did not know him very well but had met him a few times. Jack and Adrian used to play together and she had admired Adrian's finesse and grace. He was also always courteous and did not shoo her off just because she was much younger or because she was a girl.

They met a couple of times over lunch–moments to be cherished. However, for Julia, meeting Rose the first time at a party at Adrian's house was an unmitigated disaster. She found Rose snooty and uncaring. Julia found most of the others also snobbish and the kind she had been trying to avoid since coming to New York.

Adrian and Julia continued to meet for lunch every once in a while. She often thought of Adrian and his relationship with Rose. "I did make honest efforts to be friendly with Rose and their son, Paul when Adrian invited me to dinner at home, but those occasions were no better than the first visit. Rose continued to be put on superior airs and Paul seemed to take after his mother rather than the father. After two such disasters, I had made up my mind not to accept any more invitations to his house. As if reading my mind, Adrian also never invited me home after that."

They continued to see each other. Julia genuinely found being with Adrian great fun. He was such good company. They were able to laugh with each other, and sometimes at each other. They spent some wonderful afternoons together. He was fun, caring, sensitive, and honest–"everything

I always admired in a man", thought Julia to herself. Unfortunately, his wife seemed to not care about anything but herself. She felt it was such a mismatch. She made sure that their relationship was more of companionship and joy; that there was no hint of any physical closeness. In fact, it seemed to happen quite naturally. In any case, at that point, Julia was still struggling to get over her own divorce, and was being very careful that she did not get into any relationship on the bounce.

Adrian went to Julia's place after office for coffee a few times. She would play some music for him and he seemed to be completely at ease and relaxed. Such times, they would spend some time talking of many different things, or playing scrabble and then Adrian would return home.

When he told her that he was going to Chicago the following week, she was stunned into exclaiming, "This could not be coincidence!" Her own office had asked her to go the Chicago office for some work and she had been discussing dates with the Chicago office. When she went back to the office, she finalized the programme so they could go in the same flight. She was thrilled with the thought.

Julia was not a good flyer. But the flight to Chicago turned out to be quite wonderful. They were chatting up all the way.

"The first evening was a little disappointing. I was looking forward to spending the evening with Adrian. Adrian called me early evening and said that he would stuck at work till late, and that he would grab a sandwich in the office itself. I just ordered a sandwich and decided to watch a movie in the room."

The next day, however, Adrian managed to finish work early and invited her to dinner. She got ready with special care.

"What happened at that dinner will be etched in my memory forever. One minute we were talking happily, and the next there was a stunned silence. This happened more than once. It was as if external forces were acting on us, trying to direct us somewhere. At one point Adrian put his hand on mine and I started trembling, hot and cold at the same time. I looked at him, and felt myself blushing. I always thought girls blushing was a thing of the past generations, but I could feel blood rushing to my cheeks, making them burn. I suddenly avoided looking at Adrian.

Each time our hands touched on the walk back to the hotel, it felt as if a million centipedes were running all over me. I wished the walk would never end.

At the hotel, he walked me to my room, and kissed me goodnight. I had heard someone use the expression, "bells ring and the world becomes colourful when you kiss your soulmate." It was as if the words were especially written for this occasion. However, I was not just in two minds, but in several. I wanted him so badly that every cell in my body was aching for him. Yet, I knew he was a married man–however unhappily–and I respected him for his views on sex before marriage, or with anyone other than the spouse. I pulled back from the kiss and whispered, "We shouldn't," just as he said the same words. I quickly ducked back into the room and shut the door. I could hear his footsteps, walking away. I showered, changed but could hardly contain myself or steady my breathing. I knew it was right for us to be together in every way, physically or otherwise. I also knew it was not right. After being torn apart for several minutes, I picked up the phone and then put it down. Picked it up again, hesitated and finally called him on room-to-room. He picked it up instantly, and said, "I am coming over.""

She waited for him with a lot of apprehensions. But the moment he took her in his arms, she simply became one with him. All her fears, all her tensions and stresses simply vanished into thin air. It was a case of two bodies, but one soul.

"Oh, God! I never want to be away from him. My life is incomplete without him", screamed every cell in her.

ADRIAN

"After that incredible evening in Chicago, we were both subdued and excited and happy at the same time. The flight back to New York was as wonderful as the onward flight, and even more complete in a sense.

We spent as much time together as we could back in New York. The physical part of our relationship was as beautiful as every other part of the relationship. You know, I had always thought of sex as something gross. But with Julia, it felt divine. I could never have imagined that it could transcend the grossly physical to the divinely sublime.

All I wanted was to see a smile on her face, coming from deep within her. We had many wonderful moments, doing crazy things together."

"What about Rose? Did she not know about this?"

"I am not sure whether she knew or not. I did tell her that I met Julia in Chicago. But she seemed so immersed in her own activities–in her own words, "being seen with the right people at the right places." I did try to spend as much time as I could with the Paul–taking him to ball games, museums, movies etc. Sometimes Rose would join us for a movie, but most times, she had her own agenda. However, she seemed to be able to influence the kid a lot more than I could teach him what I thought were right values. Rose seemed more concerned with material wealth and social position than anything else.

After the first few months, I could not see where the relationship with Julia was going. We were still enjoying each other's company to the hilt, but I could see no sensible end in sight. Despite everything, I wished Rose well and did not want to hurt her or Paul, as I was sure would happen if I continued to see Julia. On the other hand, I wanted Julia so much, and I sensed that Julia would be shattered if we broke up. I knew she would lose faith in mankind."

Adrian was torn apart. On the one side was his legal wife, married in a church, and his son. On the other hand was everything he ever sought in life–true love, emotional bonding, and a woman who was truly a woman in his eyes. He felt truly like a man when he was with her; he felt complete when he was with her.

Many a time he went to the only source of support he knew, the church. He would go to the church at times when there was hardly anyone else there, sit in the pew and reach out to God. "Oh, Lord! Show me what to do. I don't want to hurt anyone ....."

***

CHAPTER IV

There was an uneasy silence when Adrian finished. While he himself seemed to be reliving what he had gone through, each of the others was mulling over his dilemma.

Mark said, "What you have been through is somewhat similar to what I have had to go through, although my dilemma was quite different."

Sridhar smiled, "The cause of half the problems in this world is a girl!"

"Yes," chipped in Vibhuti, "and the other half is due to men!"

There was laughter.

"Tell your story, Mark."

"I will start at the point I met Clara. I stepped out of the church, clutching my overcoat, into the biting cold. I had spent a few minutes alone in the church, trying to make some sense of life. It was cold and clammy on that Saturday morning. There was no one in sight, other than this young girl crying bitterly to herself. It was as if the whole world had decided to let her be and did not want to watch her distress. There was a park not far from the church, and it was on a bench in that park that this girl was sitting.

She looked wild, head exposed, her hair unkempt, tears flowing down the face that had no make-up. I looked at her for a few minutes, hesitated and then decided there was no point in my getting involved in whatever was troubling the girl. I just continued on.

After walking some distance, however, something clutched at me–I know not what. It felt as if I was attached to her on a spring. The farther I forced myself to walk, the greater the pull I sensed. I looked back and there she was, still in the same position, knees pulled up, hands around her knees, head lowered, weeping. I turned and walked back to the bench and quietly sat there, saying nothing. The girl continued to cry. This went on for quite a while."

"Mark was really sweet. What I liked best was that he did not say anything. His presence was enough," Clara chipped in.

"I did not really need to say anything. I felt I should allow her the freedom to get whatever was bothering her out of her system. In fact, despite the fact that I was sitting next to someone crying bitterly, I was somehow undisturbed. If there had been a passer-by–fortunately there wasn't--he would have wondered what the quarrel was about and what I had done to this girl!"

Added Clara "Till I became a little calmer, I did not even see him. I only sensed the presence of someone next to me. When I was feeling a little better, I turned to him and said, "Clara. Thank you for being there. And more so, for not saying or doing anything."

"Mark. You are welcome." extending my hand.

"After that introduction, we still did not speak. She seemed immersed in her own thoughts. Again, I let her be. Somehow, I felt calmer than I had been even after my prayers in the church. I don't know if it had anything to do with reaching out to another human being in pain.

After about 10 minutes, when I judged that she had got over the crying, I turned to her and asked if she was hungry."

"It is amazing how we connect with another human being. Here was a man I did not know from Adam, who by his own admission had walked off after seeing me in distress, but felt compelled to return, and suddenly, it was as if he was reading my thoughts. Just as he asked if I was hungry, I had realized that I was starving. Till then the thought of eating anything did not seem to be anywhere in the horizon."

"We walked to a quiet pub nearby and ordered some meat pie and bitters. Slowly, over the next several days, Clara's story emerged. I will let Clara tell you her story, while I sit back and enjoy my tea."

Clara said, "Here goes: I don't know if you any of has had the experience of growing up in a family where the parents were constantly at each other. No? I am glad none of you had to go through that. It is a horrible feeling. And I was an only child.

Both my parents were independently rich. My father was a successful banker and had inherited his business from my grandfather. I am not sure what each of my parents was looking for in life. They were good people individually, but somehow there was no 'togetherness'. All the negatives seemed to come out when they were together. I am not sure what was behind it.

I went to one of the better schools and graduated from Cambridge University. As a teenager, I had realized that both my parents were having affairs outside the marriage, and were keeping up the pretence only for show, and convenience. Even before I left for college, I too had an affair with an older man. He was keen on our getting married, but I felt quite uncomfortable and cut the relationship short very quickly. I really did not feel good about the affair.

Not that it stopped me from experimenting with other men. I also tried drugs, fortunately at a very mild level. After college, I just drifted around, attending parties, not knowing what I wanted. I was not short of funds, my parents having put aside a liberal allowance for me. Money, sex, drugs or any of the other things I tried–none of them seemed to get me to where I wanted to go. I was depressed and unhappy much of the time.

I did try going to the church, though neither of my parents were so inclined. I was hoping that the church might provide some answers. However, to say that the church did nothing to help would be a gross understatement. In fact, the church actually drove me further into depression.

I had many so-called friends. Most of them were only looking to see what they could get out of me. I knew my life was a mess, with no direction, no purpose. I would sit alone and cry several times. I ate at no fixed times, eating whatever I could lay my hands on whenever I was really hungry. I slept at odd hours. In fact, most nights were frightening, because I just could not get to sleep.

The day I met Mark, I had been wandering the streets for several hours, not caring about the cold. I ended up on this bench in the park, on which I sat and pondered over my life. Nothing seemed to make any sense. I started to cry uncontrollably. I don't even know how long I sat on the bench or how long I cried, but I sensed Mark's presence at some point. I wasn't sure I wanted anyone around, but did not want him to get up and go. The rest you know."

"You talked of questions about life. What exactly were the issues bothering you?" asked Sridhar.

"I had always asked myself questions such as 'Why was I born?' or 'What are we doing here on the earth?' –even as a growing child. My parents were of no help at all. In fact, they pooh-poohed my questions. I used to have long discussions with some of my friends at school. But these discussions never came to anything. It was clear to all of us in the group that there was more to life than making a lot of money. I believe we were an unusual bunch of boys and girls. While we did have interest in things that most youngsters have at that stage in life, we thought beyond them. I am not sure what happened to all of them later on in life. The only one I heard about was a boy called Simon, who was said to have gone to Tibet and disappeared. Apparently no one ever heard of him again. For all you know, he might have become a monk!

I saw hardships and grief among many people – even among many who outwardly were not sad. It appeared so unjust. How can a God who is supposed to be merciful cause so much unhappiness, allow catastrophes such as floods and earthquakes or even wars? Why do so many people have to suffer so much for no apparent reason?

As I grew up, I turned to the church for answers, and found that the church could not give me any satisfactory answers. In fact, all the church did was to put 'fear' into me. Mark came into my life like a floating log to a drowning person."

"What happened, Mark, after you took Clara to the pub?"

"Truth be told, I was worried about leaving her alone. I wasn't really sure she had got over whatever was bothering her. We were there for a couple of hours, mostly talking generalities. And the little bits about her life that Clara let fall. Finally, I asked her where she lived and dropped her back home. She told me she lived alone. I was still unsure about leaving her alone in her flat, but decided not to risk getting involved any more. Another round of tea, anyone?"

There was a chorus of yesses. Mark called room service and ordered more tea.

"However, I could not get this strange girl out of my head. I kept wondering why she seemed so unhappy and disturbed. I was also concerned that in the unhappy state she was in, she should not do anything drastic. That night I tossed and turned in bed and early next morning I went back to her flat. I was not sure she would be up. But by morning, my own anxiety levels about her had gone up and I had worked myself up to a state where I was really worried about her."

"Were you married at that time?" Vibhuti

"Married and recently divorced."

"Tell your story from beginning, please," pleaded Ali.

"OK. I was born in a small town in Devon and was an only child. We had a small farm and I grew up among many animals. My parents were very conventional, regular church going folk. I am not sure what the relationship between them was, but from the time I can recall, I never heard either of them address the other with love. They seemed clear about what task each had in life as well as in the farm and went about doing their duties. As I grew up, I realized that they did not even sleep in the same room. I loved to spend time with the animals and found myself happy in their company.

I was pretty much of a loner. I did not mix with many people, did not have many friends in school. My favourite hideout was a milestone about 5 miles out of town. The road was not frequented much, and the area was very pleasant. There were woods and meadows on both sides of the road. That is where most of my thoughts were formulated.

Once I observed a bird carrying a worm in its beak. It looked like the worm was trying to struggle out of the pincers. The delicacy with which the bird was carrying its delicacy awed me. I felt that the bird could easily snap the worm in two–or was it three–parts!

I started wondering what the short life of the worm was like, or for that matter that of the bird. The bird was probably taking the worm to feed its chicks. My thoughts flitted from the worm to the bird, to bigger animals, to man and to a possible ogre or giant that would eat humans and have a life span of several centuries, and then back to the cells that made up each one of them.

I had read, for example, that a moth had a life only of a few minutes–born, is, gone! In what would appear to us as a flash. Would another species like a giant with a much longer life span than that of man also think of us in similar terms?

I thought and thought. Sometimes it looked as though I had a flash of understanding–a great depth of understanding. But the momentary flash passed and I was as unsure about everything as I was in the beginning."

"Wow that sounds like one of those great thinkers, or poets, who seem to be able to see far more than we mere mortals!"

"In fact, I loved poetry and found great depth in seemingly simple poems that I came across in school or in my readings in the local library. I sensed that the poets had great depth of understanding, that they were able to see patterns and deep meaning in simple everyday things.

I myself started writing poetry by the time I was about 10. I found it easier to express myself in verse than in prose."

"Do you have any of your early poems with you," asked Adrian

"I might have some in my PC. Let me see."

Mark opened his PC, rummaged through his files and said,

"Ah, here is a small one that I like."

UNTITLED

I am but a puppet.
Who pulls my strings,
Hanging loose?
Or is it a noose?

I live, I eat, I grow,
I know not for what.
Why is two and two four,
And not twenty more?

A baby is born
Whence has it come?
The beginning endless
The end only a mess.

"You wrote it when you were ten? Incredible."

"No, this I wrote when I was just into my teens. I used to look around and wonder about the world around us. I knew stars were very, very far and I had read that space itself was expanding continuously. I tried imagining 'endless' and found myself sucked into impossible vortex of thoughts.

I found school quite boring and the teaching methods tiresome. Every PTA meeting in school gave the same inputs to my parents–capable of being at the top of the class if he puts in a little more effort. My answer was really the same every time: I see no value in doing more. I get enough to remain somewhere in the top quartile of the class.

I finished school and left home to find a job as an assistant in a departmental store in the next town. I quickly rose to be a manager. In two years, I had found a job with a large chain in London at their Head Office.

I registered for a graduate degree. I found it quite fascinating to begin with, but soon was frustrated with the inadequacies in the so-called science. I felt that most of the theories and hypothesis were built on very shaky basis and had too many exceptions. I quit after two years. I was doing well at work anyway.

After a short period of courtship, Annie and I were married. Marriage, however, was a great disappointment. We never really did find that magic in marriage. I do not know if it was because the marriage itself was an immature decision or whether we drifted apart after marriage. We found that our interests were very different, as was the approach to life. We parted company, fortunately, with no children. I dated other girls, but none extended beyond a few months.

I continued to be a loner, with very few real friends. I spent a lot of time listening to music or in contemplation, writing or sitting in the church. I did go to church every Sunday and for all special services, but I found greater solace in sitting in an empty church. I also donated my tithe regularly and participated in some of the church activities. I had a copy of the Bible in my room, although I did not read it regularly.

The day I met Clara I had spent a fair amount of time sitting in the empty church, as I often did, wondering about life and what Jesus tried to tell us. Although I did not find the answers, I did come out feeling better."

"But not as good as being with me, right?" said Clara with a twinkle in her eyes. Mark smiled, and it seemed to everyone that there was an unspoken message passing between Mark and Clara.

"So what did you find when you went to Clara's flat the following day?"

"Quite simply, nothing! I had taken a tube to Charing Cross and walked to her building. I knew from the day before that her flat was on the fourth floor of this fancy building in Covent Garden, surrounded by many theatres, boutiques and fancy restaurants.

I tried ringing her bell several times, but there was no answer. I was beginning to get a little worried. Either she was still sleeping or something worse. What I was hoping against hope was that she was up early and had gone out, however improbable that may sound. I did not even have her phone number to call.

As I was standing outside her building, wondering what I should do, I saw her at the end of the street. She was in her running gear, running towards the building. Whew! What relief flowed over me! I thought it was a very good sign that she had gone for a run early in the morning. She smiled at me dazzlingly (Mark looked at Clara who gave him another dazzling smile). I was immensely relieved.

"What are you doing here so early in the morning?" asked Clara.

"Oh, I didn't have your number. I only knew your place. Have you eaten anything?"

"Not yet. I had an orange juice before I left for a jog."

"Get ready. Let's go and find some breakfast."

"Okay. Come on up, while I get changed."

"We took the lift to her flat on the fourth floor. It was a beautiful two bedroom one, with a large reception room with a feature fire place. There was an open kitchen. I was somewhat surprised to see how well it was kept. Clara got me an orange juice from the fridge and went in to change.

I was impressed by the array of books on her shelf. Books on comparative religion, interpretation of God, self-help books, books on philosophy, including translations of Greek philosophy, some fiction. I also noticed translations of the Quran and the Bhagawad Gita. The book shelf covered one wall totally. A copy of The Prophet by Khalil Gibran was open on the table. There was no TV.

She stepped out of her room, looking fresh like a newly bloomed flower. The dominating feature, however, was her smile, that seemed to light up the whole room. What contrast to yesterday! It was difficult to believe it was the same girl.

We went to a small restaurant nearby. I ordered some eggs and bacon. She restricted herself to toast, coffee and some fresh fruits. I told her that I was planning to go to church and asked if she would join me. She refused quite categorically. "You go ahead. May be we can meet up for a bite of lunch later." I tried persuading her that it might do her good to go to church, but she was quite adamant."

"Did you go to church?" asked Vibhuti.

"Yes, I try and make it to church every Sunday. It is almost like an anchor in a world that otherwise seems to be drifting rudderless in a vast ocean. It seems as if there is no land in sight, only a vast expanse of water. In fact, the sermon was on brotherly love and he talked about being protective of each other. I started wondering if Clara aroused my protective instincts. Because I did feel very protective of her. I still do!"

"Yes. It is pretty obvious!"

"I came back from church to pick up Clara. We had lunch in a small Bistro. She was looking quite stunning in a simple green outfit that enhanced her effortless aura of a combination of simplicity and elegance. After lunch, over coffee, we sat in comfortable silence, each engrossed in our own thoughts.

She asked me about my association with the church and whether I was a 'good' Christian. In fact, then and many times later we talked of the church and what it meant to me. I tried telling her about some of my childhood and the role church played in my growing up. I dropped her back in her flat a little later, with the promise that we would meet again."

"We did. We met regularly over coffee or lunch. Sometimes we would take a scenic drive, avoiding the M roads and driving along A and B roads, passing scenic villages. Those were very special for me.

After about a couple of months, we went on a similar drive and stopped at a pub in a village."

Clara asked, "What is God?"

"To me God is represented by Jesus Christ. In Jesus I find a physical form of the Lord, all powerful, all merciful. When I am troubled, I turn to God in the form of Jesus."

"So you look to God to solve your problems? Why go to church every bloody Sunday then?"

"I want to keep my link with God at all times. Only then, when I am in difficulty can I rightfully turn to Him. Even in our normal dealings, we don't just ring up a friend after many years of non-communication, only to ask a favour. It is true that God, through Jesus, keeps a regular watch over all of us, and what we do. He knows when we have followed His wishes and when we have not. Yet, it is important to set aside some time regularly to connect with God. The best place to do that is in church.

In the church, I find certain calmness. Clearly the ambience has something to do with it, as also the fact that I grew up going to church from early childhood. "Why are you so against going to church, Clara?" I asked."

"Actually, I am quite indifferent to the church. I do not find the kind of peace in the church that people like you seem to be able to. I did try. There was a time when I thought that the church might give me some clarity. I also went to confessional. Unfortunately, instead of giving me solace, getting to church only drove me further away."

"Did anything happen to put you off?"

"It is not a pleasant memory," she said, absent-mindedly pushing peas and other bits of foods around in her plate. "And the person it came from was so unexpected that I got thrown off completely. It was at a church fete, where I had gone to help out. Those were the days when I was genuinely trying to see if the church could help me handle myself. One of the priests, considerably older than I was, tried to molest me. The first time it happened, I thought it was an accident. I did nothing. When it happened again, I made a scene. Some others had also seen what he tried to do, and it became a very unpleasant situation."

"So what happened to the priest?"

"I really don't know. I walked off and never went to church again. One could let it pass as an aberration in the church, such as can happen in any organization, there being the odd black sheep everywhere. However, The unexpectedness of it, at a time when I was really looking to see if the church could give me the kind of support I was looking for just shook me up."

Mark thought about what she said and then asked, "Going back to your original question, what to you is God?"

"I wish I knew. I can sense that there has to be some kind of power that is higher than human. However, I find it difficult to imagine this power in any form, especially in human form. I read a book where the author argues that what we call God are really aliens. He infers from cave drawings, scriptures of different religions, descriptions found in ancient texts that God could have been extra-terrestrial. I remember seeing cave drawings in the book that could be modern day space traveller. He quotes descriptions from ancient texts that could be descriptions of modern day rocket lift-off", she said, continuing to play with her food.

Mark continued.

"Over the next few months, I examined my relationship with her. I felt responsible for her, somehow. I had read somewhere that in China if you save a person's life, you become responsible for him for life! I could relate to that, even though I hadn't really "saved" her life. I knew in some fashion she had become precious to me and wished I could help her get things straight. Why could she not see how Christ could be the real solution to her problems? I did try taking her to the church with me a few times, but she seemed to be very uncomfortable. It seemed to me she came to the church for my sake."

"Actually, I did go to the church only because you wanted to go there. I had no interest and was convinced the church had no answers. By then Mark had already become my anchor and life did not seem so confusing," said Clara addressing everyone.

"That's a nice thing to say," Mark continued "I felt that if I could be around her for some more time, she would find her own purpose in life and be able to find happiness. I felt I needed to protect her, possibly from herself.

Those days Clara was taut like a violin string. If handled gently and with the right skill, she would produce wonderful music. But, any extra pressure in the wrong direction could snap the string, the backlash harming her and anyone around her at that time. The thought she might harm herself troubled me constantly.

I got really busy with my work in the office for a few weeks and did not get to meet her, although she was never away from my thoughts. One day, after the crisis at work had eased a bit, I called her and left a message for her. This was quite normal. She would then invariably call me back. However, this time, she did not. After about five calls without getting a response, I got really worried.

As soon as I could, I left the office and rushed to her flat. I knew she was in, but she did not open the door. After spending several minutes trying to raise her, I went down to the Super, and told him that there seemed to be a problem. I had been there several times and knew the Super, an old man called Harold. He obviously sensed the urgency and came with me to open her door.

The scene that confronted me was a bit frightening. She was sitting–more lounging–on the sofa, eyes rolled up, breathing with great difficulty. She also seemed to be frothing at the mouth. She had obviously thrown up, vomit all over her and on the sofa.

For the first time in my life, I almost panicked. But better sense prevailed; I calmed down, called 999. I tried to raise her, cleaned her up a bit by the time the ambulance arrived.

At the hospital, she was put on a ventilator immediately, and the resident doctor said that they would not be able to tell me anything immediately. I sat all night in the hospital, waiting. In the morning, I went to my house, had a wash and change and went to the office. Clara was still in ICU, on ventilator.

I went straight to my boss's office. I knew he was under stress himself, with the crisis not having been resolved completely. I told him I needed a few days off. Wilson–that was his name–blew his top.

"No," he told me, "I cannot afford to have you missing office at this time. You know the kind of problems we are facing. You complete the work in the next few days, and I promise everyone in the team will get time off. The next few days are still very critical."

"So is my personal life. I will spend a couple of hours in the office, and brief Claude and Tara on what needs to be done. I will also be available on phone. But I have to go, and will not be available in the office for the next few days."

"Wilson would not agree. Voices were raised. Finally, I simply left my leave application on his table and walked off. I did spend some time with the other members of the team, especially, Claude and Tara. They showed a lot more empathy than Wilson, and said they would take care of things. I was not sure what my fate would be when I got back to work. I was past caring.

I rushed back to the hospital to be with Clara. I did not even have her parents' numbers and could not inform them. I dialled the last dialled number on her phone and reached a friend called Nathan. He promised to find out her parents' number and inform them.

By the time I reached the hospital, Clara had been taken off the ventilator and moved to a private room. She was conscious and smiled as I walked into her room. I spoke to the doctor, who said they were doing more tests to find out what caused the problem. However, he said that Clara was out of danger, although they would like to watch her for another 48 hours."

"He was sweet. He stayed with me all the time, and kept badgering the doctors and nurses to find out what had happened and what needed to be done to make sure I come out of it without a scratch and that it does not recur. If you are ever unwell I would recommend Mark as the caretaker. He was really good," added Clara, with an impish smile.

"The doctors wouldn't give me much information. All they would say is that it looks like a reaction of alcohol on the prescription drugs she was taking. On my pestering, they told me that such reaction happens only in some cases, not all. I did some research on the internet and was, if anything more confused! I had to wait for her father to come to get more details.

Her father came a day later, and found out that she had been taking some prescription drugs for depression. She was specifically told not to mix those medicines with hard liquor. Apparently, that day, she was feeling very alone and took a few drinks. There seemed to have been some reaction. The doctor also said that had she not been brought in for some more time, she could have been in real danger.

I found her father a bit of a stiff. He was tall, dressed very formally as if he were just coming from a Board of Directors meeting. He had an aura of authority about him.

Clearly, he loved Clara but seemed to struggle to express it. He thanked me formally for getting Clara to the hospital in time. He had the hospital staff complete all the formalities, paid them, had Clara discharged. Clara went with him; reluctantly. or so it seemed to me. I did not get to see her for several weeks after that.

When I got back to office, fortunately, the crisis had blown over and work was back to near-normal. That means chaotic, but not critical! Claude and Tara had covered up for me well, though both went through some rough times. Wilson did not fire me (and had, in fact, sanctioned my leave), but I felt that he was only waiting for an opportunity to put me in my place."

"I owe you both big time. Thanks," I said to Claude and Tara when we met around the vending machine.

"What was the emergency?" asked Tara.

"I have somehow become responsible for a little girl I know. She was critically ill and I had to be around her till she got out of it." I said cryptically.

"Your current girlfriend?"

"Not really. But I feel very protective towards her."

"How about her family?"

"Her father finally blew in from wherever he was, after 2 days. He was all stiff and formal and just whisked her away to his country residence for rest and recuperation. I must say, though, he commanded a lot of respect, even among the doctors and other staff at the hospital."

"Where is she now? Still in the country?"

"Yes. I guess she will call when she returns."

"Were the police involved? They generally are, in such cases."

"They were. They quizzed me no end. I asked the investigating officer if it was a possible suicide attempt. He said no, there was no evidence of attempted suicide.

Nor did they suspect any foul play. They closed the case declaring it an accident.

I got a call from Clara after about two weeks. She sounded cheerful enough."

"Want to take me out to dinner tonight?" she asked.

"I was, of course, delighted. I had been wondering how she was. I picked up her up in the evening, after work. What a difference! She looked positively radiant. So much so, I started wondering if the solution for her problems was for her to stay in the country.

She came down wearing a smart dark blue skirt below the knee that, instead of making her look formal, radiated casual elegance. She had on a frilly white top that seemed to highlight the glow in her face. A simple medium-heeled shoe and a jacket casually thrown over her shoulder completed the picture."

"Wow. I am impressed! I didn't know you noticed these things." exclaimed Clara.

"Mark, I too am impressed. Men normally never notice what a girl is wearing. If I asked Sridhar what I was wearing yesterday, I am sure he would be blank! I am surprised you didn't immediately ask her to marry you." Vibhuti added.

"Well, yes. But that picture of Clara is still green in my memory. And remember, I was pretty recently divorced and not in any mood to get into another relationship. In fact, I may have been overcautious.

Also, in some fashion I felt I was in *loco parentis* to Clara. She was a little girl I had to protect from the slings and arrows of this world. Marriage as an idea never entered my mind."

Clara said, "The time I spent at the country house did me a lot of good. I missed Mark very much, but felt it was better that I use the time and freedom to think over what had been happening to me, especially in the recent past. Mark such a powerful anchor in the wild-storms of life that I felt I would find it difficult to traverse it without his support. When I got to the country house, I decided to see how it goes without Mark.

For one thing, my food habits became more regular, and the outdoors did me good as well. After the first couple of days, I also slept better than I had for quite some time. In fact, the medication I had been given may have included some to help me sleep.

Daddy spent as much time as he could with me in the country, but his work called him away very often. I restarted painting, an activity that I used to enjoy but had stopped for some years.

I thought a lot about Mark and myself, and what Mark meant to me. Interestingly, I too did not consider marriage with Mark."

"Was it because of the significant difference in age between you two?" asked Vibhuti.

"I am not sure. It may have had a bearing on it. However, I had started to look up to Mark as the stabilising element in life; like they have these things that help ships not roll over? Ballast!"

Mark continued:

"She showed me some of the paintings she had done while at her father's country house, mainly landscapes–beautiful. I don't know much about painting, but I thought they reflected a certain melancholy, a certain subtle trashing of the beauty of nature. It was as if a cruel child had used an invisible brush to deface the paintings.

She also spoke to me about her dad. It was obvious that she loved her dad, but there seemed to be an element of disapproval running as an undercurrent in each positive statement.

She was much more animated and enthusiastic when she spoke of Surendra, an artist of Indian origin who had taken temporary residence in the village."

"Hey, that's a new angle. Clara, tell us about this artist."

"I ran into him accidentally when I was concentrating on a difficult landscape that I was trying to capture. He stood behind me silently for I don't know how long. Finally, he said, "If you make the brown here more streaked, you will get a better effect."

"I was shocked because that was the precise part of the painting that I had been trying to get just right. I turned to him and smiled. He gave me one or two more ideas, and suddenly my painting started looking so much better.

I discovered that he was quite a renowned painter. I did a search on him and found that his paintings were well regarded and collectors were willing to pay significant sums for them. He was in his late thirties. He had come to England over 15 years ago and had made a name for himself in the art circles.

We spent several evening together, where he would critically appraise my paintings. He also invited me to comment on the paintings he was doing at that time, and seemed to be pleased with my comments, even if they were not positive. He had set up a large screen and would project some well-known and not-so-well-known paintings and we would discuss the plusses and minuses of each of them."

"Clara couldn't stop talking about Surendra. He seemed to have made her stay in the country house not only enjoyable, but productive, both in terms of her painting output as well as her general well-being."

"That was a very interesting phase of my life. I invited Surendra home on a few occasions, but he seemed generally disinclined. I did not press him. Overall, my stay in the country was a turning point in my life. However, I was keen to return to London and spend time with Mark."

Back in London:

"One day, out of the blue, Clara said, "I want to meet your parents."

"We decided to drive down over a weekend. The initial reaction of my parents was not negative, but when she refused to go to church on Sunday, both my parents were put off. My father spoke to me man-to-man and advised me against developing the relationship with her any further. He cautioned me that we were proper Christian folk who believed in the power of Jesus and of the church. I reassured him that there really was nothing between us and that we were just friends. The rest of the visit passed without the warmth that was there in the beginning of the visit. We returned to London and resumed our normal routine.

We continued to see each other regularly, sharing all that was happening in each of our lives. Clara spoke about the different people she met and her assessment of them. She seemed to drift towards people who would not be considered 'normal' by my parents. Each one of them was an eccentric in his or her own way!

One such was Leon Bauer, a German photographer, who specialized in human forms. He also did work with models and aspiring models and helped them create their portfolio. Clara decided to join him as an assistant."

"Leon is fantastic guy. He loves his camera as well as his subjects. When he is on a shoot, he caresses the camera and almost makes love to the subject. He is sublime. I love working with him. He is also extremely creative," chipped in Clara. "There is a large picture he has taken of a nude girl's silhouette in black and white, which I thought could easily win accolades and awards. But Leon refused to send any of his pictures for any competition, saying he did not need the approval of a bunch of non-creative people."

"When I met him, I found him quite weird. Long hair streaked with white, wearing dresses that were borrowed from many different cultures, smoking unusually short foul-smelling cigars that he imported. He had a way of talking of the human body, including such features as length of eyebrows–both male and female–in poetic terms. He had a theory that humans as we know them now will not exist in the future and wanted to preserve the current form for posterity. His creativity was, however, unquestionable.

Things had settled down to a sort of routine. Every time we met, Clara would have a new story to tell about her photo sessions. She also attended several photo exhibitions with Leon. She would come up with amazing stories of the people who came to the gallery–all her imagination, of course."

"That's not true. Each one of my assessments on people who walked into the gallery was based on solid observation and analysis." Clara.

"I tried getting Clara to hit a gym or join me in long walks or cycling activities. She was not very enthusiastic. She said, "I might try yoga."

I remember the day when Clara came for dinner all excited, literally floating in air. She just wouldn't stop talking about Suryan, whom she had met the previous day. In fact, she had called me the previous night, totally high and told me that she thought she had found purpose to life."

"Mark," she said, "You must meet Suryan. He is just what the doctor ordered! I am going to join his yoga classes."

"I was very happy that she had joined yoga classes and felt it might do her good. From that day on, she was a regular, dedicated yoga student, and every time we met she would show me what she had learnt. I had not seen her more happy and at peace with herself ever before."

"Suryan taught us today that each one of us is complete in ourselves. He used the Sanskrit word *purna*. It is amazing how much peace one can derive just by the understanding of the concept of *Bhagwan* and connectedness in the world," she enthused one day.

On another day, "*Ahimsa* is the greatest virtue. *Ahimsa* means not hurting another being physically or emotionally. Anything that causes any form of hurt is *himsa*. Did you know that Jain monks cover their mouth and nostril with a piece of cloth to minimize the harm they cause to bacteria they might inadvertently breathe in?"

And again, "Surya says that the answer to all our questions and doubts lies in the *Vedas*. It helps us respect nature in all its aspects and pray when we do anything that might hurt another living being, including plants and trees. This is because of the essential oneness of everything in this universe."

Suryan says, "You are the whole, the Being, the *Atma* and all else is only a projection."

"What about her work with Leon?"

"She continued to do that. In fact, continues even now. But, every time we met, Clara was full of Suryan, yoga class (which obviously extended beyond contorting the body!) and Hindoo philosophy. It was usually "Suryan this, Suryan that" and "Suryan said..." The good thing was that I felt that was the best period for Clara. She was joyful and looked radiant."

"She looks radiant even now!" exclaimed Adrian.

"Sure she does. She seemed to be veering towards a religion that I did not even begin to understand. I felt sad that the religion she was born to, one that seemed to help me so much, was not the one she found comfort in.

One day, she called me and said, "Mark, come home. I have something wonderful to show you!"

I bought a bottle of fine wine and went to see Clara at her home, wondering what new surprise she had. I found she had prepared a small pedestal and was ready to install an image of a man with a peacock headgear and a flute in his hand. "This is Lord Krishna," she said with great respect, handling the image tenderly. "Isn't he beautiful?!"

The image was captivating. It looked very old, was made of ivory and was about 6" tall. There was a mischievous smile on the face and he had one leg crossed over the other ankle. "Who is it?" I asked."

"Lord Krishna is the destroyer of evil, protector of the good, one who bestows his grace on his devotees and fills their lives with joy and happiness. He is one of the Hindoo Gods."

"Many questions flashed through my mind. How can she fall for this kind of idol worship? How can she let go of Christ and hang on to an image that seems no more than a piece of art? How can an idol do all the things she says He does? How does this piece of ivory give her so much joy?

"Isn't ivory banned?" I asked latching on to what was perhaps the least important of the questions, which she ignored.

Clara placed the idol ceremoniously on the pedestal she had created. She then placed a few flowers at the feet of the idol and then, with obvious sincerity, she bowed to the idol.

Another time she called me home, all excited. When I went there, there was another girl, an Indian. But what took my breath away was Clara, looking like a doll, dressed up in a yellow *sari*, with a dot on her forehead."

"How do I look?"

"Elegant ..., graceful ..., stunning ..., Wow!"

"This is Asha. She taught me to wear the *sari*."

"Hullo, Asha. Mark."

"Yes, I know. Clara can hardly stop talking about you! We are together in the yoga class."

"Clara then said that they were going to a Hindoo temple and insisted that I accompany them. I was getting increasingly concerned about the way Clara was going, but could not help feeling happy at seeing how happy it made her. I was torn between shaking her up and telling her to get real and wanting to be with her to enjoy the wonderful feeling her happiness brought out in me. Should I now let her be and not feel protective of her anymore? Should I simply allow her the total freedom to do what she wants and just bask in the beauty of her being?

I did go the temple with them but was totally confused at all the rituals, which seemed to make no sense. How can so many people not see that a stone image is but a stone image? How can any religion permit worship of idols and images? God could not possibly be cast in any form, I have been repeatedly told.

Clara and Asha participated in the rituals enthusiastically. I could not bring myself to do so. At one point, the priest doled out small spoonsful of water to all the people and they actually drank the water! I just kept in the background.

The girls seemed to pray with a lot of devotion, but I did not find the atmosphere conducive to prayer.

As the days went by, I watched helplessly as Clara continued to get deeper and deeper into the Hindoo religion. I visited temples with her because she wanted me to, but could still not bring myself to pray there.

All the while, I realized I was getting attracted to Clara in ways that very different from how our relationship was in the earlier stages. I think I was beginning to fall in love with her, without my knowing. I found joy in everything she said or did, and my only goal was to see her happy, all the way from within. I felt her ideas were strange, but that did not deter me from wanting to please her and see the smile on her.

She seemed to have given up all her western dresses and had taken to wearing *saris*. I must confess she looked fetching in that dress and the dot on the forehead seemed to add certain lustre to her. She also began to read the Bhagwad Gita, which she said was the best guide to correct living. I accompanied her on her visits to the temple, even though it went against all I had learnt.

I went to my parish priest, one who I could confide in and told him that I thought I was falling in love with this wonderful, but strange girl. He heard me out and said that what she was going through was like a disease and hopefully she would be cured of it soon. It is like the many fads youngsters go through and when she sees the true picture, she will drop this nonsense. He strongly advised me to be with her, to try and help her get over the infatuation, but to not entertain any thoughts of marriage with her. He suggested that it would actually cause me confusion and harm, and would not do her any good.

He told me that I would rise enormously in the eyes of the church and Christ if I could help get her back into the fold."

"Mark was sweet," interjected Clara, "he never refused to accompany me to the Krishna temple, even though I knew he was troubled. I knew I could not lose Mark. I tried my best to not force any of my understanding of the Hindoo religion on him and did not discuss it if he did not want to. I don't know when it started to dawn on me that I was desperately falling in love with him and did not want him to leave my side even for a moment. If he had shown the least sign, I would have fallen into his arms with a "yes" on my lips. I knew he was troubled with the differences in our perceptions about religion and how life should be led. I had turned totally vegetarian and that made it difficult for even to go out to dinner together. However, I was getting deeper and deeper into what I was certain is the right way to live. It became clear to me that the ancient seers, *rishis* of India knew something that we did not.

After one of his visits to India, Suryan talked to us in the yoga class about his trip, about the great men he had met in places like Varanasi and Rishikesh. He fired up the imagination of several of us. We all planned to go to India for a vacation. However, I did not want to go without Mark."

"Clara talked to me about India and the richness of its culture. She told me she wanted to go to India with other yoga students, many of who were going to travel with their spouse or boy/girlfriend. "Please come with me to India," she said.

By that time, I could refuse her nothing, nothing at all. I had some leave due and a trip to India did sound fascinating. The opportunity to travel with Clara was something I did not want to miss. So I told her to go ahead and make the itinerary and that I would be delighted to go with her.

We landed in Delhi, went to Agra and Jaipur–fascinating places all, though rather unclean. Then we travelled to Rishikesh, Allahabad and Varanasi. I was happy just looking at Clara joyfully immersing herself into what to me seemed entirely alien activity. I was overwhelmed seeing her bathing in the sacred, but dirty river Ganges and taking part in the *puja* and other rituals at every temple.

By the time we returned to London, I was convinced that Clara was the only girl for me. That I wanted to raise a family with her and spend the rest my life with her.

I went back to the parish priest and talked to him again at length. I explained to him my feelings for Clara and that I could not conceive of life without her. He was sympathetic, and asked if she had formally converted to Hinduism. I told him that as far as I could make out she was a pukka Hindoo, and that she had stated clearly that when she gets married, it will in a Krishna temple, with Hindoo rituals. He cautioned me again about marrying outside the church. He went on to say that it is a sad thing that one born in the church had drifted so far away. His advice was unambiguous.

I was torn asunder. Our relationship had transcended the earlier one and got deeper and much more meaningful. It was clear that neither of us wanted to live without the other, but the differences built a Great Wall of China between us. Neither of us was comfortable moving in with the other.

The following year, Clara again wanted to visit India and this time wanted to do a round of the southern part of the country. Among other places, we also wanted to visit the Sai Baba Ashram in Bangalore. I had met several people in London who swore by Sai Baba. He seemed to have great powers to cure illnesses that the medical fraternity had given up on, and also bring peace into the lives of people.

That visit was the one that brought us to Visalam."

"Wow, what a story! Life certainly has no shortage of excitements, problems, dilemmas, crossroads and its ups and downs. As I listen to each of the stories, I sense that we have been brought together for a purpose–and that feeling is getting stronger and stronger. I am sure Ali has an equally interesting tale to tell us?"

CHAPTER V

"I not make love story, like Adrian and Mark. My story is for my son, Asghar.

We live now in difficult time. Unnecessary. Man make his life more difficult by dividing himself, separating human to human. Adrian and Mark talk about their religion. I also very religion. I good Muslim and pray to Allah as told in Quran. Why man use religion to fight and kill everyone is crazy. No religion can say go and kill. We make territory like animals and fight like animals also. I also see many people one-to-one are very good for another person, no religion come into relation. But when we together, we call many names for us and fight. For what? I not understand.

I caught in such cycle. I peaceful man. My country generally good and peaceful. The king–may Allah shower his blessings upon him–is kind and we live good.

But, I Muslim. Many Muslim from other countries come to us and use us. Allah is kind and will help them also. But these people create many problems."

Ali stopped, choking a bit and there was heavy silence. Vibhuti got up and gave Ali some water. He took charge of himself and continued.

"I want more people like Lady Visalam everywhere. Another people also help many and bring peace in their life and in the community. We need more, more more people like this in all over the world."

He paused again and after taking a deep breath, continued.

"My brother, Hassan, I, we are happy family. We have good food, Allah be praised. We pray regularly and give to poor also. My country has much oil that the America and Europe want, and we have good life. Our King make university, hospitals, and also factory. Only our weather is very hot. He smiled.

Allah is great and merciful. He will save all of us. Many prayers to Allah for peace in world. Many brothers think wrong. There is no need to kill anyone to make him believe in Allah. It is silly. Allah never say kill. I want everyone in the world be happy. And to be happy, they have to pray to Allah. I let them pray in their own way. They will finally find Allah and then happy. I am no need for force anyone.

Holy Quran is good book for living. Everyone can follow the Holy Quran. But there is no force. I want to help all. I tell all they should pray to Allah to be happy. But I don't kill them if do not.

I study Holy Quran for many years. My teachers are very good. I have also thought deep about it. Holy Quran not say kill people. Holy Quran say 'show them way to happiness'. Many Muslim read the Holy Quran wrong. And also take young men away from truth of Holy Quran. They tell them wrong things. They tell them others are *kafirs*, must be killed. Holy Quran not say. They brainwash young men to kill themselves, kill many others. They tell you will go to *Jannat* if you kill them. No! Wrong! Holy Quran not say like that.

More recently, after my experiences in India, I am thinking that may be other Gods also guide people. I still think prayer to Allah is the way to live life, but other people may also have good idea. All dedicated people will at end find Allah.

In India I find another people also like Lady Visalam who can give peace to people and community. Many very good people, also my doctor in the hospital. They don't turn away because I am Muslim. If more people like Lady Visalam there in all over the world, we will be better people, not fight."

Ali seemed to be immersed in his own thoughts, furiously fingering his prayer beads. Vibhuti got up and served more tea. "Ali, like the others, why don't you also tell us your story from the beginning."

"Yes. We are happy family," he said, looking at his brother, "A big happy family. I grew up in the town of Bulwa learning all about Islam and studying Holy Quran. I go to Madrassa to learn *alef-be*. I go to mosque regularly, every *jumme* and also pray at home other days. I like people and discuss many things with my brothers and friends. When I become 21, I marry my cousin, beautiful girl Zahira. We lived very happy for two years and then become more happy. Zahira was becoming mother – and I am proud father.

One day, Zeenat, my sister-in-law come running and crying. "Zahira is very bad," she cries, "please come quick." I run to Zahira and see she very ill and many blood on floor. I panic, call ambulance and we rush to hospital. They take

Zahira to operation theatre. I wait, praying to Allah all the time. After many hours, I don't know how many hours, doctor call me."

"Ali. I give you some good news. You are proud father of a healthy boy. But, I am sorry, we tried best to save your wife. We could not do anything. She died on the operating table." I not sure what to think.

"I love Zahira very much. I am joy to be father of a son, but Zahira died. I not sure I should cry or be happy. Zeenat take care of my son. We stay in hospital for some days and then go home. My son, Asghar. I call him Asghar. Beautiful baby. He look so happy. He is all I have. I not marry again. I will spend all my life helping Asghar, be with him all time.

I happy to spend as much time as possible with Asghar. He say first word, Ma, but no mother. I father and mother for Asghar. Asghar is happy. He learn all. When he try to stand up, I am really happy. I thank Allah everywhere.

"Come, Asghar jaan, come to Baba," I try to help him walk, a little first, and then I go backwards and he keep walking to me. When he fall, I rush to him, gather him to me, hug him, sing to him. But Asghar not cry even if he fall badly. He is ready to get up and walk again. First he cannot walk. He fall down every time. He cleverly holds one table and then wall and he walk to me. It is so nice–my son Asghar and I.

When Asghar is more than two years, I start to teach him *alef-be*. I give him Holy Qoran, even also he does not read. But Qoran his first book, the best book. I teach him respect for holy book.

I take him to a Madrassa near house. I know the mulla and discuss many Qoran with him. He is good man, noble man and good teacher, but very strict."

"Whole life is in Qoran," he tell me one day. "Nothing outside holy book."

"He take Asghar as his student and teach him everything – Holy Qoran, science, mathematics, religion, economics, political science, geometry, medicine and also making many things by hand.

This was good, because I not able to spend much time at the home now. I also have to travel. I spend much time as possible with Asghar and happy he is learning from good teacher. Asghar also make new friends. "This is good," I tell to myself, "he must be with friends like his age."

I see he grow quickly. I watch proud. Asghar slowly become a big, strong boy. He is quiet and concentrate on his studies.

"How is everything, son?" I ask one day.

He tell me, all fine. He studying hard. Most time when I am home, Asghar busy with his work. He does not go out to play much. I also happy that he keep his Holy Qoran with him and take good care.

Some times on *jummeh*, I take Asghar on picnic. He is happy to come with me. Sometimes he go on long walk only himself. He tell me he want to be alone with nature.

One time, we are in picnic in the mountains. Our country has much mountains and rivers. It is beautiful, very good for picnic. The weather is cool and nice. Asghar run after a wild chicken. Kwa, kwa, the chicken runs. Asghar run after chicken. Laughing. I am very happy to see Asghar laugh open like that. Suddenly, Asghar trip over stone and fall and start to cry. I rush to him and hug him and wash his wounds. I tell him it is nothing, only small scratch. Asghar calms down. But I worry. I heard somebody say small scratch can also make big problem. I want to go back and see one doctor. But Asghar is happy to run around again.

On way back, he ask, "Abba, are all person's blood same colour?" I think it is very good question. I tell that there may be only small differences in shade, but all blood is red. He knows a lot about man body, even if he is only small boy. He read a lot and ask many questions about everything. When we go back, I take him to doctor and ask to check and give him injection. Make sure there is no infection. All the time Asghar seems only amused.

I take good care of Asghar's food. I not want him to fall ill. He is strong. But, one day, when Asghar was about 9 years, I came home and found Asghar have fever. His body very hot. He is struggling to breathe. I very worried. I ask Zeenat and others what happen. They only say he came from playing and went to sleep. But I know he is very ill. I shout at all of them they don't take care. I take Asghar quickly to hospital. They check him and immediately ask him to be admitted. They want to make some tests. I very upset with everyone. Later, doctor tell me that Asghar will be taken to ICU. He is not able to breathe properly. How can anything happen to my Asghar. He is Allah's gift, perfectly healthy. I ask doctor many question. Only Dr. Kumar talk to me properly. He tell me that Asghar is very unwell, but they will do everything to make him alright. I ask what is problem. He not sure, but say test result will show. He think Asghar have infection. What infection, I ask. He tell me that is what they are trying to find out. Have you given him any medicine, I ask. Yes, he is on antibiotic and medicine to reduce the temperature. They also help him breathe better in the ICU. Asghar look so small and helpless in the hospital bed, with many tubes. He is also connected to many machines. Doctor make me sure he is looked after well and he will be OK in a few days.

"Allah, you are great, you all powerful. You know everything. You are also mercy. Why make like this for Asghar? He is good boy. He read Holy Qoran every day." I ask forgive if I do anything wrong. Don't punish Asghar, please.

For two days I stay with Asghar. I ask all doctors to say he is OK. But Asghar look very weak and pale. I no eat food, no talk to anyone, not go for work. Zeenat and other people come to hospital. I no listen to anybody. I pray all time. Doctors come many times, nurses come and test his temperature, write something in their book. Nobody tell me my Asghar will be good. Only Dr. Kumar say, "Don't worry. We do everything possible. We will make him OK. Only pray to Allah."

Then Asghar open his eyes and smile at me. I am very happy. When he go back to sleep, I rush to prayer room and pray. I say, "Oh, mercy, Allah. Thank you. I know you also love Asghar. Please make him well very soon. If you take him away from you, I cannot live after that. Please make him normal, happy. If he is suffering more, how can I continue to pray to you?"

For another day, I was with only Asghar in the ICU. Then the hospital move him to another room. The entire time, my whole world was only my son; there was nothing else in the world. Only Asghar and then Allah. Slowly, Asghar recover and become like himself. I am joyed. I thank everybody in the hospital, specially Dr. Kumar. The day he was allowed to go home was a wonderful day. There was some rain, as if Allah tell me that all is well and throw his blessing on Asghar and me. As we come out of the hospital, everything was looking very beautiful. I sat in car, hugging Asghar and praying to Allah, the great, the powerful, the forgiving.

The next years good. Asghar was generally near the top of the class. He used to ask me a lot of questions. Some I am able to answer, many others I did not know. But I was very happy that Asghar is showing many interest to learn new things. His teachers were happy and always gave him a good report.

Around the time he was 14, I started to notice changes in him. He became more quiet, stopped asking so many questions, spent many times in his room working on the computer. He was a natural athletic, and was doing good sports. But around that time, he did not go to play many times with his friends or be part of school sports.

When I asked him what he was working on in the computer, he started to give not correct answers. I also noticed that he would close his computer quickly if came to his room without notice.

I felt that I was losing connection with him and felt sad. I thought because he was going through to become man. But I prayed to Allah that he should not go away from me. All the years I have tried my best to be father, mother, friend, teacher–everything to him. I felt he was moving away. I hoped that he would return to being the same Asghar.

I also noticed he had one or two new friends whom I did not know. When I asked him about them, he did not tell me correctly and was sometimes irritated."

Ali paused. He seemed to be reliving the time he considered the beginning of his troubles, although he was hoping that it would only be a passing phase. The others let him be, and the silence stretched taut. It seemed to Vibhuti that unless something is done quickly, it might break with a great snap, and the backlash could hurt not only Ali, but the others in the room, like the whiplash of a stretched spring that suddenly snaps. "Oh, God, what difficulties has each one passed through," she thought to herself. "Why does so much sorrow descend on people who are clearly 'good' people."

"Shall I order some more *chai*?"

"I will have a coke, with lots of ice, please." Adrian

Mark said, "Why don't we take a break and go down to the Coffee Shop. We can continue when we return."

All of them trooped down to the Coffee Shop, and then some of them decided to take a short walk, even though the weather was not really very pleasant.

When they all gathered back in the room, Ali continued.

"I sensed the distance between Asghar and me growing like a rubber stretching. He sometimes use words that were not very respectful. He sometimes called me old man and said my ideas were old fashioned. His reports from the school were not as good as they used to be. This was big worry for me.

I tried to meet Imam to discuss my worries about Asghar. He listened patiently and said, "Continue to pray. Asghar is clearly going through the phase in his growth that every boy goes through. That is a very difficult time, both for him and for the father. If you do not tell him anything, he feels that father does not care. If you try to tell him that you understand what he is going through, he feels that no one can understand what he himself is trying to grapple with. He will be OK as he grows up."

"I tried best to show that I understand his situation. But Asghar listened more to his new friends than to his father. And some of them the cause for his increasing disrespect for elders, I am sure. He seemed surly most of the time.

Around this time I accidentally came to know that one of our neighbours, Arif was part of a group trying to plant a bomb in a crowded market in another country. I knew him, but not intimately. As far as I could tell, he was a quiet person and kept himself to himself. He came to the Masjid regularly and followed the prescriptions given in the Holy Qoran–his commitment to Allah, or regular prayers or fasting. I not know what he do otherwise. I was not sure what I must do with the information I had got about him by accident. I thought ask him directly. But I think that not right. May be I should give information to police, but I not have much trust in the police. Or, I just forget it. Finally, after many days of agony, I go to our Imam and tell him what I knew. "Good you told me," he said, "I will take care of this problem. You don't worry about it anymore."

A few days after that, Arif was arrested as he stepped out of the house and taken away. Asghar was there when this happened and was upset. "He was a good Muslim. I see him regularly at the masjid, praying with full heart. Why should he be harassed?" I told him that he has gone with police to help them with something illegal someone else had done. Asghar looked unconvinced, but not say anything.

I got back to my life and my attempts to be the father and mother and everything to Asghar. I desperately want him to be the son I seemed to have lost. I wanted to hear him say, "Baba, you are the best teacher," as I had heard him say earlier. I wanted to laugh with him, play with him.

Many of his new friends I not like. Many I not even know. Earlier, he would bring his friends home to be with him, to eat with us, to study together. That seemed like another age.

Vacation time was good time for us. But slowly, he seemed more interested in spending time with his friends during vacation than go out with me. That summer vacation, he said he wanted to spend time in the house of a friend in the mountains. He said some other friends will also be there to spend time together doing things like trekking, and other adventure sports. I thought a change may help Asghar and reluctantly agreed.

I know recently we not spend much time together, but still I missed him when he went away. There was emptiness in my life and I was hoping Asghar felt same way and come back soon. I did everything mechanically, all the time hoping and praying that the change would bring back old Asghar; I imagined him running and hold me tight (he was big man now) and "Baba, I missed you!"

But Allah did not wish it that way. Asghar came back after 4 or 5 weeks, and was still aloof. However, I notice that there were changes. He was more alert than before. I also thought he was become more sure of himself.

The good news was that he continued to study the Holy Qoran and kept his copy of the Holy Book close to him. Bad news was that all that I had taught Asghar about love seemed to have evaporated into nothing.

"People need to be saved from themselves and from others," he told me one day, "Allah is the only way to do that." Another time, "the world is divided into two classes of people-one who follow the Qoran and live life as dictated by Holy Book, and the other who are either fools or unwitting accomplices of forces against the correct and righteous." Yet again, "There is only one religion and only one Allah. Soon the whole world will follow us." Paraphrasing something he probably heard elsewhere, "You are with us or, if not, then against us."

He appeared especially bitter about Jews and Hindoos. I know historically we have problem with Jews and Christians, although all three religions come from the same origin. But, Asghar think that Jews and Hindoos are the cause of all problems for the followers of Allah. We had several discussions on the Holy Qoran and I tried to tell him that main precept of the Holy Book is love. He not agree, argue that the Holy Qoran specifically tells the faithful to bring everyone to Islam, by love or, if necessary, by force.

I tried to make him understand that others may follow other religions now, but on their own they will eventually come to Islam. We have to do nothing other than explain. He said, "Baba, you realize they are all sinners? Do you not know that only accepting Islam will destroy all their sins?" Quoting Qoran 3:85, he said, "If anyone desires a religion other than Islam, never will it be accepted of him; and in the hereafter, he will be in the ranks of those who have lost their selves in the hellfire."

I discussed with him Chapter 25, which talks only of love and peace. But Asghar kept saying such thinking of no value in world of today. It is an evil world and will trample upon those who go by such 'soft' ideology. "Baba, you interpret wrongly. It says clearly that whatever Prophet Muhammed said later overrules anything said to the contrary earlier. This principle is clearly stated in 2:106. And if you read all that has been said later, when Prophet Muhammad and others were in Medina, it becomes clear that the Prophet has commanded all followers to ensure that Islam is the superior religion, in fact, the only religion. All others false."

Our Imam was a very scholarly and powerful man in the country. I asked Asghar to meet him and discuss his views with him. However, Asghar found reasons and excuses to not meet him and discuss with Imam his understanding. When I spoke to the Imam, he only said, "Let him be. Soon he will understand himself."

This continued for some time. I kept praying and hoping that I would get back old Asghar, bubbly and look to his Baba for everything. I was away for a couple of days and when I returned, I went looking for Asghar. When I went to his room, he introduced his friend. "Baba. This is my friend Sharief. I would like him to stay with us for a few days."

I was not sure how long he had already been there. I took an instant dislike to Sharief. I did not think he was good company for Asghar, but I felt powerless. The two of them stayed up till late. I could hear them talking softly for a long time.

The next day I found both of them gone. There was no note or any message. Asghar did not return by night and I started to worry. That evening, I was sitting watching TV without watching; wondering why I am being put to so much distress. Something in the TV caught my attention when I saw what looked like a somewhat blurred picture of Sharief. I was not sure. I had seen him only for a few minutes, but something did strike me. I turned up the volume to hear what it was about. What it was about only made the situation that I thought could not get worse, much worse.

There had been a terrorist attack in another country a few days ago, killing several people. I had heard the news, but did not pay much attention to it. Now, it appeared that one of the suspects was a person who looked like Sharief.

My health began to fail and I could no longer think straight. To make matters worse, a few days later, the police came to my house asking for Ali. Allah forgive me; I lied to them that I had not seen Ali for several days and had no idea where he was. When they showed me a picture of Sharief, I again lied that I did not know who he was and that I had never seen him.

I am clearly not a very good liar because they decided to take me to continue their interrogations. This was not good news, because I had heard stories of people being taken in for questioning and never heard of again. As we were leaving the house, I asked one of my neighbours to inform the Imam.

The day I spend in custody was very terrible. I was put in a solitary room, with no windows and not allowed out at any time. I was not given any food or water and had to urinate and defecate in one corner of the room. The already smelly room was becoming intolerable. A bright naked bulb burned in the room at all times. Sleep was impossible.

Many people came to question me, using different methods. Some would tempt me by saying that I would be freed if I told them where Asghar was. Some stuck terror in me, painting a picture of what would happen to me, if I continued to tell them the same story. Sometimes they would use a belt to beat me. I survived only because I had faith in Allah. I stuck to my story that I had no idea who was in the picture they showed me and that I had not seen Asghar for several days.

Fortunately, the next day I was released. Our Imam was waiting outside for me, along with my brother. I kissed his hand and fell at his feet, whimpering. They took me home and after a bath and some food, slept for several hours. When I got up, I pieced together the story. My neighbour had gone to tell the Imam about my being taken away, but he was out. As soon as he returned, he had apparently taken charge and used his contacts to get me released, standing personal guarantee for me. I always had great respect for him; now he seemed to be Allah's own messenger to me.

I went to see him later in the day. He questioned me closely about Asghar. I had always been open and honest with him, seeing in him my guide. For the first time, I could not bring myself to tell him the truth about Asghar. I lied to him, Allah forgive me. I could not betray Asghar. He was too precious to me; he was everything to me.

I guessed where Asghar might have gone. I have half-sister in remote village on the mountains, where I had taken him once when he was a young boy. His aunt and he seemed to have found an equation and able to communicate to each other. Although he had met her only once, I knew he must have gone there. The place was so remote it took days to reach the village from the nearest town. There was no road, only a mountain footpath. She lived in a ramshackle hut and ran a farm of sorts.

Ali went silent, and there was palpable disturbance in the air. It became clear to everyone that Ali had had to undergo something no one should have to–implicate his beloved son, the only reason for his existence or give up everything that he himself stood for.

CHAPTER VI

"*Adiye, panchaptram uddarani yengai?* (where are the vessels for my prayers?) Ramachandra Iyer was waiting in the open courtyard of the small house, waiting for his things to be brought to him for his daily *puja*, prayers. It was a small single storey house with two rooms and a kitchen, in a row of similar houses in an *agraharam*, on a secondary street of Kumbakonam with a temple at one end of the street. Everyone in the street belonged to the *brahman* community who tended to be orthodox and convention bound.

The houses had common walls. They had heavy doors that were generally kept open. There was no concept of 'bedrooms'. Everyone slept on a mat made of woven straw, with a sheet and a pillow. In the morning, everyone was expected to roll up this 'bed' and put it away in one of the two rooms. The other room was generally used as the 'drawing room', where visitors were entertained. The drawing room had two plastic chairs and a teapoy. The two rooms and kitchen formed the entire house, except for the open courtyard behind each house. In the courtyard was a tap for washing utensils and a well for taking bath and washing clothes. At the end of the courtyard was the toilet.

Kamakshiamma, wearing a traditional 9-yard *sari* quietly brought all the ingredients and placed them in front of her husband and master.

Mr. Iyer was an assistant to the *gumasta*, a lawyer's clerk. Typically, such clerks ended up doing multiple tasks, as record keepers, scribes for petitioners and others who came to the lawyer, and other miscellaneous tasks. They were treated as 'hey, you' and worked for a very small salary. However, his family and his peers considered it an honourable profession and he was happy doing it, mainly because he could read and write. Mr. Iyer had no great ambition and was happy with his lot.

At 34, he had been married for 14 years and had a daughter, Visalam.

Later that night, after she had served her husband his dinner, Kamakshiamma shared the remains with her daughter Visalam. Then she carried a tray of betel leaves and areca nuts to the room, where Mr. Iyer was reading the newspaper. This was part of a daily ritual for Ramachandra Iyer. After a few minutes of chewing noisily, Iyer asked, "Hmm. What?"

"I think Visalam has had enough of school. It is time we thought about her marriage." Very shyly, very hesitantly.

"Why, did she do something to cause you to worry?"

"No, but she is already almost a big girl and needs to focus on learning things that will serve her better at her husband's house. She is almost ready for motherhood."

"Ah, I know what you mean." said Ramachandra Iyer with a twinkle in his eyes, "Why don't we give her a baby to mother? She can learn easily!"

Kamakshiamma covered her blush with the ends of her saree.

A year later, a beautiful baby girl, Lakshmi was born to the couple. However, Kamakshiamma developed complications at childbirth.

***

Visalam was overjoyed. She loved the baby and did everything for her. Lakshmi was the doll Visalam never had to play with. She stitched her clothes, and spent all her free time with her.

She also cared for her mother, who was now bedridden. She took over all the household work, in addition to going to school. Her father also needed looking after, which responsibility also fell on Visalam. As her mother continued to deteriorate, she stopped going to school after completing the Class X examinations.

"Trrrrrrrrrinnng....." The alarm went off. Visalam looked up to check the time – 4:30. It was still dark outside. She was up in a jiffy and went to take a bath. She cleaned the bathroom, washed her clothes and, went to the prayer room. "*Sarve bhavantu sukhinaha, sarve santu nirmayah; sarve bhadrani pashyantu, ma kaschit dukhabaag bhavet*" as final her prayer for the morning.

On a typical day, Visalam woke up at 4:30 AM, and after a bath and finishing her prayers, used cow dung to clean up the front entrance to the house.

She looked at the kolam (pattern drawn at the entrance to the house, using rice powder) she had drawn with satisfaction.

"Time for Amma's bath," she said to herself and went in. "How are you feeling Amma," she said, undressing her. She had brought some warm water and a sponge and gave her mother a sponge bath. "I could not sleep well again. I tried my best to repeat *Isvara's* name till I finally fell asleep and slept fitfully."

"You will be alright, Amma. The doctor has given you very good medicine. In just a few days, you will be in the verandah, playing with Lakshmi," she said reassuringly.

She heard her father going to the bathroom and hurried to the kitchen to make his coffee. She drew bath water for her father and while he was at the bath, fed the baby, bathed her and got the things ready for his morning prayers.

While her father was getting ready, Visalam quickly got her puja plate ready. She walked the short distance to the temple, greeting her neighbours on the way. She did not wear any footwear as she had, in any case, to remove them at the temple's main entrance.

As she entered the main portal, she bent down to touch the doorstep and touched her forehead in a gesture of obeisance. The magnificence of the temple never ceased to amaze and awe her. The *gopura* (tall towers that rise on the walls of temples at the entrances) on the entrance walls were immense and represented the feet of the Lord. She looked at the brilliantly painted carvings and felt a sense of elation.

She reached the inner sanctum, admiring the *vimana* (tower erected over the main sanctum sanctorum of temples in southern India). There are usually excellent carvings on the face of the *vimana* that rose high into the sky, as if inviting the Lord to descend into the sanctum sanctorum and bless the devotees. Visalam handed over the garland of flowers she had managed to stitch together to be put at the feet of the deity. The priest recited some mantras, showed camphor light to the deity, and then returned a small portion of the garland to Visalam, which she took with reverence and put on her hair. She circumabulated the deity and returned home in time to cook food for everyone, and see her father off to work.

She then sat with her mother and spoon-fed her food, wiping her mother's mouth often with the end of her half-sari. (This dress, common in many parts of Southern India, is worn by young girls transiting from a skirt to a sari).

She played with Lakshmi and taught her prayer verses. After eating her food, she managed to get a little rest.

In the afternoon, she again fed Lakshmi, spent some time with her mother. She washed all the clothes, including those of the baby. That was only time she had available to clean and dust the house.

Before her father returned from work, she lit two oil lamps for the Gods that had been set up in one corner of the room and recited some prayers. She kept the baby with her, so she could also learn the prayers.

There was no cooking oil in the house and she was short of vegetables for the evening meal. She decided to get them before her father came home. Visalam went to a neighbour's house and requested the young daughter to be in her house and play with Lakshmi while she went to the market to get a few things. She readily agreed.

Visalam stepped out and went to the street corner shop in the next street. This was small shop set up in front of the house.

"Namaskaram", she said to the girl at the shop in greeting, "how is Amma doing?"

"She is much better. There is no fever now, *Akka*."

"Good. I am sure she will be OK soon. Can you give me half kilo of *til oil*, please." She took a basket from the shop and selected some potatoes, beans, bitter gourd, coriander leaves, curry leaves and ginger. She gave these to the girl to weigh and cost. After paying her and thanking her, she went home quickly.

When her father came back from work, she prepared coffee and tiffin for him. She then prepared his prayer things for his evening prayer.

Later, she cooked dinner, and after serving her father, fed Lakshmi and her mother, helped her mother go to the bathroom. She played for a while with Lakshmi, continuing to teach her some basic mathematics and prayer mantras and, then put her to sleep.

She spent some time with her schoolbooks, although she had stopped going to school, before completing her *japa* and then going to sleep on her mat on the floor.

***

"Amma, are you alright?"

"Yes. I can hear Lord Krishna calling me. He has such a beautiful smile!"

Visalam touched her mother's forehead and found she had very high fever. She ran to the kitchen to get some cold water from the pot, wet a cloth and started to try and bring the fever down. She asked a neighbour to call the doctor. All the doctor could do when he arrived was to pronounce her dead.

With a lot of help from neighbours, Visalam organized the funeral. Having depended on his wife all his life, and then on Visalam for everything, her father was of no help. He left everything to be organised by Visalam.

Mr. Iyer really took very little interest in anything other than the daily rituals he performed punctiliously. He had no great attachment to daughters, not even to the baby, whose birth was the starting point for his wife's death.

The men folk had gone to the funeral. Visalam was in the house with some neighbours and a few relatives who had come for the funeral.

"Akka, what happened to Amma?" Lakshmi.

"She has gone to be with Isvara, God."

"Will we also go there?"

"Eventually everyone has to go there. We are all created by God. And what is created must eventually re-join the creator," said Visalam, amidst sobs.

***

Mr. Iyer was beginning to be concerned about Visalam's marriage. Without Kamakshiamma, he was lost. This was not a subject he could discuss with Visalam, who had taken over the duties of her mother. He had already given her horoscope to a priest he knew, to try and find a good match for Visalam.

It was a Sunday. After finishing his morning meals, Mr. Iyer took his umbrella and walked to buy himself some tobacco to chew. It was hot, well into the forties, but Mr. Iyer was quite used to the heat. There were not too many people on the streets. Even the street dogs seemed to eschew the sun and find a little shade to get over the hot part of the day.

The roads were generally clean, even if chaotic. Most main roads had shop fronts that tended to be different from each other. There was a large poster of a James Bond film in Tamil, right next to another poster that depicted Lord Krishna in a religious film. There were a few *petti kadai*, shops run of small box-like structures selling items of daily need. Many of them had bottles displaying different sweets and a series of satchels handing from a string tied across the shop, ranging from shampoo to coffee powder to Lay's chips.

There were several temples on the way, most of them closed till evening. Some of them were grandiose, and some were small street corner temples. All of them, he knew, were old–several hundred, if not thousand, years old. He knew the priests of some of these temples. Many of them had large water bodies attached to them.

The biggest such tank is the Mahamham tank, attached to the Adi Kumbeswarar Temple, located in the centre of the town. Legend has it that Lord Shiva, dressed as a hunter, shot an arrow at a pot (*khumba*) held by Lord Brahma and broke it. It was a celestial pot containing nectar and where the nectar fell became the Mahamaham tank. It is said the name Kumbakonam derives from *khumba* (pot) and *konam* (crooked).

Kumbakonam has many experts who could cast and read a person's horoscope and predict the future. More importantly, they would assess if a marriage between a boy and a girl would go well by matching the two horoscopes.

Mr. Iyer decided to go and see the priest whom he had asked to find a match for his daughter and see how far he had come in the search. Mr. Iyer entered a small lane behind one of the many temples in the city, and knocked on the door of the priest's house.

After the initial generalities, the *vadyar* (priest) said, "Mr Iyer, I have found a good match for your daughter. Their horoscopes are well matched. Good family, has a good job with the Railways, and no bad habits." The *vadyar* continued to extol the virtues of the boy, "He has done BA. You should invite them to come and see the girl." Mr. Iyer agreed and set a date for the visit.

A fortnight later, the priest brought Raman and his parents to visit Mr. Iyer to see the motherless girl.

"She is good girl and knows all the household work. She has, in fact, been managing the house now for some time on her own. She looked after her sick mother better than a professional nurse could ever have. Have some MysorePak (a common south Indian sweet). Visalam made it with her own hands." The priest was now singing praises of the girl. After some discussions regarding the families, they talked about the wedding itself and what was expected of Mr. Iyer. The wedding was fixed for five months later.

For the first time in many years, Mr. Iyer took some responsibility and went about making the arrangements.

His brother, who was a school teacher, came to help him. They arranged for the wedding to take place in a temple which had a suitable area for it. The guest list included about 80 close relatives and some friends of Mr. Iyer. They also arranged for the guests who come for the wedding to have lunch at a nearby restaurant. The wedding went off without a hitch.

At the end of the wedding, Lakshmi wouldn't let go of her sister, clinging to her as if her life depended on her. "Akka, don't leave me and go!" she wailed. Her father gently pulled her away to allow Visalam to go. Visalam too, was reluctant to go, although she was hopefully going to a new, exciting life. She turned back to her father and hugging him, sobbed uncontrollably. She picked up her little sister and reassured her that she was always there for her and would be in close touch.

Almost dragging her feet, she went with her new husband, looking back often, with tears still streaming down her cheeks.

***

Three years into the marriage, there was no child. "What is wrong with you, girl. Can't you even fulfil the basic duty of a woman? Where is my grandson?" chided her mother-in-law.

Raman was tall, thin individual, with no aspirations in life. He started as a small time clerk in the Southern Railways, soon after doing his BA and stayed more or less at that level, with the small increments that come one's way in a steady Government job. He had little outside interests, except eating sweets. Despite the large amounts of the extremely sugar-rich Indian sweets, he remained thin as a reed.

"Mr Raman fainted in office and has been taken to the Railway hospital, There is nothing to worry about," said the peon who came from Raman's office one day. Visalam dropped everything she was doing and rushed to the hospital. Raman was stable, but the doctor told her that his sugar was high and that he would have to take care to eliminate sugar from his diet and to do regular exercise, including walking for at least an hour a day.

Visalam began to innovate in the way she prepared food for her husband. While she was willing to share the same food, her mother-in-law needed what she called "good south Indian food." Visalam ended up making separate dishes for her mother-in-law.

After the first few days, Raman could not resist sweets and started having some at the office, secretly. He also baulked at the idea of having to go for long walks, and avoided it using any excuse.

Soon, he had to be repeatedly admitted in the hospital and started missing work frequently. He exhausted his leave and often had to take medical leave without pay.

Visalam's mother-in-law became increasingly cantankerous and loudly started blaming Visalam for everything–absence of a grandson, her son's illness, lack of money in the house...

"Since the day you entered this house, there has been nothing but disaster. And what did your father give you in dowry? Nothing!" she screamed.

Both to avoid her mother-in-law and in the hope of bringing in some money, Visalam started to go for typing and short-hand classes.

***

Vibhuti – "It was a tough time all round. There was apparently not enough money to run the household. *Perimma* had to scrounge and save what she could but it was obviously not easy. She applied to several places for a job. While waiting for a possible job, she would hone her secretarial skills by trying to write the English radio news in shorthand. She became very good.

Amma told me that she rejected a few offers, including one very good offer as Secretary to the Director from a company that was marketing chicken. She eventually joined a small private company. Even now when Mom talks of that period, I can see she feels really bad for *perimma*."

***

One day, when Visalam came back from work, she noticed that the box of sweets someone had given them the day before had a few pieces missing. On persistent questioning, Raman admitted to taking 'one or two'.

"Amma, please help by not allowing him to eat sweets. Doctor has said that will be the death of him."

"It is your fault. Why did you leave sweets here to tempt him? Eh?"

Raman's mother died of a heart attack and the funeral organization had to be done by Visalam, although several relatives from near-by villages had also come. Visalam overheard comments like, "She has been nothing but bad luck." "They were a pretty happy family, with the son doing fairly well." "She is also barren. What woman can live with herself like this?" "Now she pretends to help the family by going out to work!"

Visalam launched herself into her work. But problems with Raman continued, with increasing leave of absence without pay from work and his inability to stop eating sweets.

"I have left food for you in the room. Please don't eat anything else," said Visalam as she left for office, "you can make yourself some coffee, without sugar. I have left the decoction ready. Just heat it up."

"Sure. I will take care of myself."

But he didn't. Eventually, Visalam had to lock him up in one room with food and other things that he may require during the day when she was at work. She was very unhappy, but there seemed to be no other solution. She continued to pray for her husband.

***

"What a tough life she has had!" exclaimed Mark. "We think we have had it tough. But, boy, compared to what she had to go through, our lives are rosy."

"I also believe that she was a special person and all this was a test for her; and to make her mature, so she could be there for others like us when the time came," Sridhar remarked.

"Most of this I heard in bits and pieces from my mother," Vibhuti said to her new-found friends. Their stories had been fascinating to hear. It was clear that the common thread of their link with Visalam bound them all.

"I will give you the complete picture as I got it from Mom and from granddad. There may be gaps till the time I was about 6. But poor *perimma*'s troubles seem unending!"

***

Visalam returned to her father's house after Raman died. She knew she could not manage at her in-laws anymore. They had made her unwelcome in many ways. Now, Raman's relatives as well other ladies insisted that she should be shorn of her hair and given only white clothes to wear. She refused and there was a tense period, when it appeared that they would force her. Fortunately, when she told them that she had to return to her father as he needed her to look after him, they did not stop her.

She was distraught for a while, and spent a lot of time at prayer, both in the house and in the temple. She took care of the entire household work, as before. She managed to find another job in Kumbakonam, with Row Fine Parts, a company that was a supplier to a multinational company called Qubec Technologies. At work things went well for her. It was a good company, with good pay and working conditions.

Lakshmi had grown to be a fine young woman and was doing well in school. She was a bubbly girl, who dreamt of finding Mr. Right. She dreamt that they would be very rich and well respected in society.

As she finished high school, Mr. Iyer told her that it was enough education for her.

"Appa, but I want to go to college. All my friends are going. One day, I will be a successful professional."

"That is not a girl's role in life. The important thing is for you to raise a good family."

"But Appa...."

"No, and that is the end of this discussion."

She ran crying to Visalam.

"Akka, I want to go to college. I don't want to be another door-mat housewife," she cried. Visalam was quiet for a few moments. "You are, of course, an exception. You are a wonderful person and have handled what life threw at you very well!"

"I will talk to Appa. And make him agree to send you to college. But as a precaution, please ensure that you dress very conservatively."

The next day, after giving her father dinner, and his betel leaf and araca nut, Visalam broached the subject with him. "Appa, please allow Lakshmi to go to college. Times have changed and the world has changed with it."

"If she studies further, it will be more difficult to find a match for her."

"She is a good girl, good looking, well-mannered, knows all the household work. It will not be difficult to find a suitable boy. Let her finish her graduation."

"Girls should get married at the right age. If we delay it very much, not only will the society think there is something wrong, but she will also have more difficulty adjusting with the in-laws," said Mr. Iyer. And to his mind, that was a clinching argument.

Eventually, Visalam convinced her father, using her own case as an example of something that they did not want Lakshmi to go through.

***

"I love you, Laks," exclaimed Vasu, "and I want to marry you even if it means I have to face the whole world." They were sipping coffee at an outdoor restaurant.

Lakshmi and Vasu met at a college fest, where she was participating in a play and he was the main organizer. They had started to see other regularly, and, over time, got really attached to each other.

"My father will never agree! I love you with all my heart and want nothing more than to spend the rest of my life with you. My family is very orthodox and when they come to know that you are an Iyengar, my father will throw a fit."

"I too will have a fight on my hands in my house. But together, we will overcome all odds. Nothing or no one is going to keep us apart."

"My only hope is my sister, Visa. She is a fantastic person, even if she is very conventional. She is the one who got father to agree to my going to college."

Laxmi and Vasu were anticipating difficulties with the families because they belonged to two different streams of Brahmins in Tamil Nadu--Iyers and Iyengars. Both believed in the supremacy of the *Vedas*, the original scriptures, but followed somewhat different understanding. The main difference is that the Iyers follow Advaita, a singular truth of all, Iyengars follow a principle of dualism, separating the individual from God. In practice, however, the difference lies in the fact that Iyengars consider Vishnu as the form of God, while Iyers pray to Shiva. Interestingly, while Iyengars generally do not go to any temple other than Vishnu, Iyers tend to be more open to visiting any temple.

These philosophical differences aside, traditional Iyers and Iyengars are strongly against marriage between the two groups. Neither would approve of such a marriage and sometimes, the opposition can be quite vehement. Clearly, both Lakshmi and Vasu had a fight on their hands.

"Akka, you have to help me. I am in love!"

"Who is this lucky boy? Do I know him?"

"No. We met two years ago. He graduated on top of the class from another college. Vasu is fantastic and is incredibly in love with me, just as I am with him. But, I am afraid to tell father."

"Very good. Are they Brahmins?"

"Yes. But Iyengar Brahmins. That is the main problem."

Lakshmi arranged for Visalam to meet Vasu. She found him a good person and judged that his love for Lakshmi was genuine.

Visalam went to Swami Atmananda, whose lectures she had been listening to from time to time, and asked for some time. She posed the problem to him and asked him for advice. Later, she also took Vasu to see him. Swamiji told her, "In today's age, it is not often that one finds a boy as sincere as this boy appears to be. Even if they are Iyengars, and you are Iyers, there is nothing in the *Sastras* (scriptural texts) to forbid such a marriage."

By now, Visalam was the de facto head of the household. Mr. Iyer had started to depend on her for almost all decisions. While be objected to the alliance, telling her that it was her decision to allow Lakshmi to go to college that had brought them to this state, he let Visalam take charge. It did not take too much effort to convince her father that this was a good marriage.

Lakshmi and Vasu were married as soon as Lakshmi finished her degree. Vasu had already got a job as a software engineer with a private company. They were happy together.

About a year later, Lakshmi came to Visalam, excited. "Akka, guess what? I want you to be the first one to know!"

"What?"

"I am going to be a mother!!!! I am just coming from the doctor's."

"Wow. Wonderful. You better start being careful. Where are you planning to have the baby? I want to be there. Does Vasu know?"

"Not yet. I am just going to call him."

"Hi, Vasu. Guess what. I want you to come home early today."

"Why? What special dish are you cooking up? I have a departmental meeting at 3. Should be over by 4. Will try and leave then. Give me a hint."

"No. I can't tell you on the phone."

"Hey, is it what I am thinking it is? Tell me yes!"

"I will only tell you in person. Come soon."

Lakshmi came to her father's house for her confinement. Visalam was all over her. "Don't sit in one position for too long," "Walk regularly," "Don't strain yourself," "be gentle with yourself.... And the baby!"

Vasu and Lakshmi had already booked a small but very efficient hospital called Mother and Child.

***

Visalam went to see Swami Atmananda.

"You look like a child who has been bequeathed an ice-cream factory!" Swamiji smiled, as Visalam prostrated before him.

"Swamiji, I am excited. With your blessings, Lakshmi's marriage has been happy and successful. She is expecting in three months."

"My blessings. I am sure she will have a divine child."

Visalam could hardly contain her thrill. She brought beautiful pictures of Gods and Goddesses to adorn the entire house. "Every time you open your eyes, it must be to see God," she told Lakshmi. Lakshmi had brought a DVD player. Visalam went and got all kinds of chants and slokas, praising this God or that, or asking for blessings, or praying for the welfare of everyone around her. She offered special prayers to her *ista-devata* (God of her choice) so that the new baby would be born healthy, beautiful, and divine.

"Lakshmi, Swamiji is giving a series of talks on Bhagwad Gita next month. I want you to come with me. I want the baby to hear God's words and learn, like Abhimanyu."

After a couple of days of listening to the lecture, Lakshmi asked her sister, "Akka, Swamiji said that one should only do what is to be done and not be concerned about the result. If everyone worked like that how will there be any progress or development? All scientific breakthroughs have come about because someone had the vision AND the ambition to achieve what he set out to achieve. We would not be where we are today if these people had simply said that they would not worry about the result of what they do!"

"We have been invited to a small dinner on the last day of his lectures. Why don't you ask Swamiji then?"

Lakshmi was lucky to get a personal audience with Swamiji at that dinner and she raised her doubt, Swamiji seated her near him and said,

"Gita does not tell you not to set a goal. By all means set yourself the toughest goals. Use all the skills and, the experiences you have to achieve it. Do course corrections. Having given of your best (including taking help from anyone who can), realize that the result is not in your hands. Hundreds of factors go into any event occurring or any result to fructify. Of these, we only know a few. Even of the few that we do know, we have no or at best, partial control over most of them. How then can one claim the result? There is an *Isvara*, the giver of *karma phala*, fruits of your actions, who controls what results should accrue and when.

Gita simply asks one to recognize the presence of *Isvara* everywhere, and as the controller of the *karma phala*. *Karma* is wilful action; *karma yoga* is doing this action with this clear understanding. Therefore do *karma yoga* is what Krishna tells Arjuna. And all of us."

On the way back home that night, Lakshmi was feeling elated. She had been in the close presence of a *Mahan*, a great soul, and had been able to clear many doubts. "Swamiji is surely a mahatma. What clarity he brings!" she told her beaming sister.

The next day Lakshmi went into labour and delivered a beautiful baby girl. Visalam was the first one to hold the baby and sensed divinity in that child. "Vibhuti," she whispered, the cry coming from the core of her being, "you are the manifestation of the glory of *Isvara*."

Visalam took a few days off to be with Lakshmi, and then with the baby. On the day she returned to work, she bought a large box of sweets and distributed to everyone in the office.

***

The bond between the new born and her aunt was unmistakable. If she had colic, it was her *perimma* who took care of her; when she got cantankerous; the person who could calm her was her aunt; when she refused to eat or created a fuss eating, only Visalam could cajole her into eating. When Lakshmi was ready to go back to work, she would leave Vibhuti at her father's house and then pick her up on the way back in the evening. Visalam would hurry back to be able to spend a little time with her.

"Wake up, beautiful," said Vasu, carrying a cup of coffee for Lakshmi, "Today I made coffee for my princess."

As they were sipping coffee in blissful silence, Vasu said, "I will be back early today. Be ready for a night out – just us. I want to spend the evening together."

"Vasu, I love you. You are the most wonderful thing that happened to me! I will speak to Akka and have Vibhuti stay over there."

Every time, Vasu and Lakshmi wanted to go out on their own, it was very convenient for them to leave Vibhuti with her aunt. Both aunt and niece were delighted with this arrangement.

When Vibhuti wanted something special, she would ask her *perimma* and be sure of getting it – whether it was a toy or a special treat.

Vibhuti grew up to be a truly divine child. She was sensitive and was friendly with everyone; and trusted everyone – almost to the point where her mother worried she might think of the wrong kind of person as a friend. She learnt many *slokas* and chants from her *perimma* and had a reverence for God. Visalam would take her to the temple as often as possible and tell her stories of the great Gods and Goddesses.

She was the pet of the entire neighbourhood. She was free with everyone, irrespective of the age. She would walk into any neighbour's house and they would welcome her.

Visalam's entire life revolved round Vibhuti. One day she came running into the house crying. "*Perimma*, I fell down."

Visalam washed her minor scratch, and put a Band-Aid. And the said, "when you get hurt, your should say, "Boo-boo, go away," and it will go away."

Vibhuti was very happy with her aunt and loved the way she seemed to make everything OK.

***

When Vibhuti was about two and half, Mr Iyer died peacefully in his bed. Only the previous evening, he had told Visalam that his life had been fulfilled, and with the new baby in the house, he had enjoyed the status of grandfather and that he was perfectly willing to go to God. "In whatever manner he wills it," he had added.

Suddenly, Visalam felt alone in the world, with no interface between herself and the unknown. Her only solace was Vibhuti. She felt her life mission was to see that child happy, grow up to be a happy person, find fulfilment in life and in marriage. She was sure Vibhuti was divine. She displayed a sense of equanimity seldom seen in such a small child. Visalam observed that Vibhuti was happy with everyone and, even more importantly, even people with sadness in their lives seemed find some happiness in the child's presence.

The child would call everyone her best friend. She reminded Visalam of her own childhood.

"I have to go and buy some provisions. I will take Vibhuti with me," said Visalam as she prepared to go to the market. Vibhuti was very happy to go with her *perimma*, who always got her what she wanted.

On the way, they saw a dead body being taken by pallbearers to the funeral home. "Why are they carrying a cot?" asked Vibhuti. Visalam explained that the person had died and that they were taking him to the cremation ground so that he could be cremated with all the rites and rituals as prescribed in the *sastras*. Vibhuti was curious. "Like what happened to *thatha*?" she asked.

"Yes."

"What happened to *thatha*?"

"He was old and had finished all that he had to do in this world. He died peacefully, a happy man. All of us will grow old and eventually die."

"Has he gone to be with God?"

"Ye........s. He will return to earth in another body."

Such conversations were common between Visalam and her niece.

"Why do we pray to God?"

"When we have exhausted all possibilities of using our own strengths, we turn to someone who has more knowledge and strength than we do, don't we? If you find difficulty in your homework and you don't understand, what do you do? You go to Amma and ask her because she knows more than you do, right? God is all-knowledge, all-power. It is only natural that we should turn to Him when we don't know what to do."

"But we go to the temple every day, even when we don't really need anything from God?"

"Very good thinking! That is right. If we do that we will not get into a situation where we have problems. Why not avoid the problem altogether?"

"That is why I also pray every day in Mummy's puja room."

"Who is your favourite God?"

"Krishna!" exclaimed Vibhuti.

"Would you like your own Krishna to pray to?"

"Wow. That would be super! I want a big one."

"How big?"

"Mmm............, at least as big as your face. And you know what kind of Krishna I want?"

She stopped in the middle of the road and stood in the classical Krishna pose – erect, with one foot on the toes, across the other, flute in hand, with a benign smile on her face.

"That is beautiful," Visalam exclaimed. "I will get you one exactly like that."

***

"Guess what, Laks. My promotion has come through! I am now a Manager and have to take over one of the units in Hyderabad. Get ready for some celebrations," exclaimed Vasu one day.

"Wow, fantastic! When do we have to move?"

"I have to take over sometime next week. I will come back in about two weeks and then we can plan the move."

"This is thrilling. But you know who will be most disappointed? Vibhuti. She is going to miss Akka something fierce."

They decided to spend the weekend with Visalam and break the news gently to her. Visalam was distraught when she heard the news, but took it philosophically. "Hyderabad is not very far. I can take an overnight bus." She consoled herself. However, her sadness at the thought of not seeing Vibhuti for weeks on end was visible.

***

"Hullo my *thangam*, how are you today?"

"You know what happened in school today, *perimma*? My friend Rajat was scolded by the teacher."

"What did he do?"

"He was being naughty in class. Wouldn't stop talking even when the teacher told him twice."

"That's not nice."

"And my friend Radhika nearly fell off the bus."

"Oh, how did that happen?"

"She was standing near the door ready to get down when the driver stopped the bus suddenly. She fell down."

"In the bus?"

"Yeah. Her knee was badly hurt. Girija Ma'm told the driver to be careful. You know a cyclist suddenly came in front of the bus, and the driver had to stop quickly. There was a first-aid kit in the bus. Ma'm cleaned her knee and put a Band-aid."

"Did you tell her boo-boo to go away?"

"Yes, And she felt better immediately."

This was more or less the trend of conversation they had every day. Vibhuti would tell her all the stories of her school, including her own feelings and thoughts. Visalam would ring her every day, despite the fact that it was a significant expense for her. She would also travel to Hyderabad as often as she could just to spend the weekend with her *thangam.*

She had meanwhile, learnt the use of computers, specifically Microsoft Word, Excel and PowerPoint.

"I am coming next weekend! What can I get for you?" asked Visalam one day.

"I want Mysorepak!" screamed Vibhuti.

"How many?"

"So many," she said, putting the phone down and spreading her little hands wide.

"I can't hear you."

"Oh, I was spreading my hands wide to show you how many I want."

"OK, Got it."

Visalam arrived at Lakshmi's house the following weekend with two bags – a small one containing her clothes and a second one for Vibhuti.

"What is in the other bag?" Lakshmi.

"A special gift for my little darling." she said, hugging Vibhuti. She excitedly opened the bag to find it full of Mysorepak.

"Wow. *Perimma*! You are the bestest."

Later that night, Visalam and Vibhuti were sleeping in Vibhuti's room. Whenever Visalam was around, Vibhuti insisted on sleeping with her *perimma*–from the time she was a small baby. As she grew older, that was the time she would share her deepest secrets with Visalam.

"Who is your best friend?" asked Visalam.

"Sudha."

"Does she also do as well as you do in school?"

"Yes. And she is also a good at sports."

Visalam had searched for and found an image of Lord Krishna exactly as Vibhuti wanted. It had not been easy. She had tried several shops, but none fitted the image she carried in her head of what she thought her Vibhuti wold like. Finally, she managed to connect with the person who makes these idols through one of the Government owned shops and ordered one exactly as she wanted.

The next day, they installed the new Lord Krishna in the prayer room, in a special place, all for Vibhuti's Krishna alone. Vibhuti had invited some of her special friends the first day's puja.

She had asked her mother to make a special sweet for the puja.

"Hey, why don't we use the Mysorepak that your *perimma* has brought?"

"Yes. I am sure Krishna will also love that."

After the puja, she distributed this *prasadam* to everyone.

"*Perimma*, this is Sridhar, Sudha's brother," she said, introducing a tall, athletic looking boy. "He is a great badminton player. One of the best. Sudha and I often go to see his matches."

Visalam met Sudha and Sridhar several times during her visits to Hyderabad.

Visalam spoke often to Lakshmi and was happy to hear that her life was pretty much on even keel. She and Vasu had quarrels as do many young husbands and wives, but always made up. Both of them were happy that Vibhuti had found such a wonderful relationship with her aunt.

"I am glad Vibhuti relates so well to Visalam. With neither grandparent alive, she would have lost out on a lot of things but for her," said Vasu one day, when talking to Lakshmi. "Vibhuti is truly a wonderful girl."

"I know. She is a really sweet thing. I wonder which of the two us she takes after. Not you certainly, not after the way you fought with me last time!"

"Nor you. You are a wild cat! And I love you."

"I love you, too. Vibhuti has really taken after Akka."

"Tell me a story, *perimma*."

"No, you tell me what you have been doing all these days."

Vibhuti and her aunt were ready to sleep.

"Nothing very special. We had a maths test last week. I told you about it. I got full marks. Sudha sang in the assembly one day, when there was puja in the school. Oh yes, Sudha and I went to see Sridhar play at the State Championships. He is a wonderful player. So graceful on the court!"

"Did he win the match?"

"He beat a player ranked above him in the quarter final. And gave a tough fight to the State Champion in the semi-final. He would have beaten him too. But they made him play both his matches on the same day. Very unfair. You know, *perimma*, he can also sing very well."

"Is he learning carnatic music?"

"No, but he picks up very fast, just hearing Sudha learn and practice. And he can sing old Hindi film songs very well. Especially, old Talat Mahmood songs."

On another visit, Vibhuti is very excited. She talks non-stop of Sridhar's being selected for a team going to China for a tournament. "He is fantastic. He beat some of the nationally ranked players and got into the team to go to China. He even beat one of the Chinese players in the tournament. He says the Chinese players are too good. He says he learnt a lot on the tour. He was also impressed with the equipment they have."

"And what does he think of Chinese girls?" teased Sudha.

"They look very funny. Even on the badminton court, it sometimes difficult to make out if it is mixed doubles match or men's doubles or women's doubles! He bought himself a new pair of shoes. Chinese made, of course, but very good."

"*Perimma*, don't forget my birthday on the 27th. I am inviting a few close friends home. Amma is baking a cake for all of us. You will be the guest of honour, where no adults are invited!

Visalam asked for a day off on Friday to combine with the weekend so she could be with Vibhuti on her birthday. She had to work long hours for a few days before that to ensure that there was no pending work that could hold her back and briefed another girl so she could take charge on that Friday.

"Happy Birthday," everyone said in chorus as Vibhuti cut the beautiful cake and blew out the candles. It was obvious that Sridhar stood out even among the young crowd. He was quiet but always ready with a smile. On Vibhuti's request, he sang some old Talat Mehmood songs, to the delight of everyone.

***

"*Perimma*, I hope you are coming to Hyderabad next month. I want you to take an additional day off on Monday. I want to take you to see Sridhar play."

"Where?"

"This year's National Badminton tournament is here. Sridhar is also playing. His match is likely to be on Monday."

All weekend, Vibhuti didn't tire of talking to her aunt about Sridhar and his preparation for the Nationals. She took Visalam to Sudha's house and showed her Sridhar's cupboard, full of trophies.

By Sunday, Sridhar had advanced to the quarter final where he was to meet a nationally ranked player called Gaurav. Vibhuti came back excitedly from school and told her aunt that Sridhar's match was scheduled that evening.

She insisted that Visalam should come with Sudha and her to watch the match. "Sridhar needs all the support he can get."

The first game was an easy one for Sridhar's opponent. He won 21-12 with some really good smashes from the back of the court. Vibhuti and Sudha continued to shout encouragement till they were already hoarse. However, Sridhar fought really hard in the next game, raising his game another notch, displacing Gaurav with some deft placements and deceptive shots. They were neck-and-neck all the way. "18-all," said the chair umpire. And then 19-all.

"20-19."

The next point was another long rally, this time Sridhar picking up some incredible smashes and managing to get back into position to retrieve the next shot as well. Eventually, Sridhar hit a beautiful cross-court drop smash, that Gaurav put into the net. "Go, Sridhar, go!" screamed Vibhuti.

Sridhar was calm, seemed oblivious of the surroundings or the spectators. His total concentration was on the shuttle and on the opponent. He won the next two points with some high quality badminton.

"One game all." announced the umpire.

Sridhar tried his best in the third and final game. However at 15-all a long rally followed, where both players moved the other all around the court. Sridhar smashed down the line from the right court, leaving Gaurav struggling to reach the shuttle.

"Out," said the line umpire, stretching his hands wide.

"That was on the line," shouted Vibhuti and Sudha together. "Cheating." Vibhuti yelled. Gaurav asked for time for the court to be wiped. After that, Gaurav brought his experience into play and reeled off the next 4 points before Sridhar could win a point. 20-16. It was too little, too late.

Gaurav won 21-16.

Vibhuti burst into tears, sobbing into her aunt's shoulder.

As they were going home, Vibhuti was all praise for Sridhar. "You were fantastic. If the line judge had not cheated in the third game, you would have beaten him."

"That was a crucial point," conceded Sridhar, "he just ran away with the game after that before I could recover."

"Did you see the racquet he was using?" Sridhar asked, "It is a fantastic new one that Yonex has come up with. Very expensive."

Later that night, talking to her aunt she said, "I wish he had won. He is such a terrific player. And so graceful on the court. He barely seems to lift his foot a centimetre off the floor as he glides around the court. What do you think, *perimma*?"

"I think he is a very good player, very calm and very focused. His power of concentration was visible during the game, especially on difficult points. He will certainly do very well."

A few days later, Sudha and Vibhuti were in Sudha's house, talking, when Sridhar walked in. "Hi, what is going on?"

"Nothing, just girl talk."

"Anna (a respectful term for elder brother, in Tamil), you are looking tense. What is wrong?"

"Nothing."

"Oh, come on. I know you too well. You can't hide anything from me."

"Just wondering how I can get hold of the new Yonex racquet. It is really good, but very expensive. If I can somehow get one, I am sure my game will improve."

"How much does it cost?" Vibhuti.

"Rs. 32,000."

"Wow, That IS expensive!"

Over the next few weeks, every time Vibhuti met Sridhar, he seemed be not his usual cheerful self. On being pressed he told her that he has somehow got to get that racquet if he is to hold his ranking.

"The distributor has arranged a special deal for State ranked players in the Academy. We need to pay only half the cost immediately, the rest in 4 interest-free instalments. Even that is too much for me."

Vibhuti told her *perimma* about the new racquet and that Sridhar was feeling depressed because he could not get himself it for himself.

That evening Vibhuti spoke to her mother about wanting to gift Sridhar the new racquet for his birthday. When Lakshmi heard the price, she told Vibhuti "Are you mad or what. Go and concentrate on your studies. You have exams coming up shortly."

A few days later, Sudha told Vibhuti that Sridhar continued to be depressed. Many of the State ranked players had got the new racquet and he says their game has improved significantly. He is afraid he might lose his ranking.

Vibhuti could not get the thought of somehow getting the racquet for Sridhar out of her mind. It seemed to occupy all her thoughts. She did not know whom to turn to. She had talked to her *perimma*, and told her that her mother refused to pay any attention to her need. Visalam advised Vibhuti to ask her father. Her father, however, deflected her saying simply, "Ask your mother."

Vibhuti knew she couldn't convince her mother.

"*Perimma*, I have to get the racquet for Sridhar. I can't see him so despondent, and losing what he cherishes most–his State ranking. He has been working so hard to raise himself to a national level. I really can't think of anyone else, *perimma*. You are my only hope. You have never said no to anything I asked for. This is perhaps the one thing I most want. Will you get it for me?"

"*Thangame*, you know I don't have that kind of money. Why don't we buy him a really good T-shirt?"

Visalam could hear the disappointment and actually feel the dejection in Vibhuti, even across the distance.

Visalam felt like crying. As was her practice in times of trouble she spent a lot of time in the puja room, concentrating her entire being into a pleading with God. However, for the first time, she did not find clarity.

She looked at her meagre savings – really nothing. She debated whether she should ask her boss for a loan. She had been well regarded in the company, and her work was appreciated. People dealt with her with respect for her personal values as well as for her dedication to and efficiency at work. She felt no one would understand why she would want a loan for such a purpose. Nor was she willing to lie to get a loan. She considered selling some of her things. But she lived frugally and had almost nothing by way of jewellery.

Some of her colleagues noticed that she was preoccupied. Some small errors crept into her work – errors that would normally never have appeared. In one instance, her boss wanted to draw some cash from the bank. He asked her to fill a cheque for him to sign.

"Is everything OK, Visalam? I notice you look a little troubled," said her boss when she took the cheque for him to sign. She had crossed a self-cheque! Blushing, almost in tears, Visalam returned to her desk, made out another cheque, went to the bathroom and had a quiet cry.

Her closest friend at work was Lata. They would meet and eat lunch together, often sharing what the other had brought.

"What is wrong, Visa? You look shattered."

Visalam explained what had happened that morning with the cheque.

"Over the last few days, you have not been yourself. Come on, unburden yourself. You will kill yourself this way."

"I can't bear to see the child unhappy. I will give anything to bring happiness into her life. Vibhuti means everything to me."

Visalam went on to explain the background and why she had to somehow raise 32,000 rupees in the next few days. "Even if I can raise 16,000 rupees, I will somehow manage the instalments."

"Did you ask boss?"

"No. It would sound silly if I were to tell him that I want to buy an expensive badminton racquet for my niece so she could gift it to her friend!"

"It's easy. Just say you need for a wedding in the family. No one will question you."

"No, I can't take a loan on a lie."

"You are really impractical, Visa. You know there is another way. We have talked about it before. Everyone claims medical expenses against false bills. It is the norm in our company. You are the only one I know who refuses to make this claim."

"You know I can't do that. How will I live with myself?"

"Look at it this way. When you negotiated your salary with the company, did they tell you that your medical bills up to a fixed limit will be reimbursed to you?"

"Yes."

"Did they also tell you, you could accumulate this limit over several months and claim against a major expense?"

"Not explicitly, as I remember. I found this out later on."

"Right. What they meant was this was part of your monthly salary packet. That is why most people claim it whether they actually spend it for medical expenses or not."

"No, it still feels incorrect to me."

"I know you are straight as an arrow. But this is really silly. If you won't, you won't. Okay. How about this? You have access to quite a lot of cash. You need the money only for a short-term loan. Why not just 'borrow' from GM's funds and return it as soon as you can. It would not be stealing. More like a short-term interest free loan. The company owes you at least that much for all that you have done."

"How can you even suggest such a thing, Lata? I will never do such a thing. Besides, just say, something happens before I can return the money, then what?"

"You are really difficult to help. I can see the pain in you and the intensity of your desire for Vibhuti's happiness. I feel sad to see you like this."

That evening Vibhuti called. "*Perimma*, Sridhar's birthday is not too far away. Have you been able to find a way?"

"Not yet, *Kanna*. I am still working on it. What else has been happening?"

"At the moment, my head is full of only this. Everything else seems so insignificant. *Perimma*, you are my only hope."

"I will see how to make this happen."

Visalam felt as if she was being torn asunder. She went back to her prayer room and sobbed her heart out. "What do I do, Krishna? I can't let her down!"

Next day in the office, Lata met her and said, "My God, You look as if you haven't slept all night! Are you alright?"

"I couldn't sleep. I spoke to Vibhuti yesterday and could not stomach the unhappiness in her voice. I prayed almost all night. I HAVE to find a way of getting her the racquet."

"I know a doctor at a clinic who would give you the necessary bills for a small fee. I have been getting them from him regularly. Come with me after office and we will solve your problem. Really, Visa, by doing this, you are not cheating anyone. In fact, by not doing anything you are only cheating yourself and Vibhuti; and in the process, making Vibhuti unhappy. You just come with me. I will take care of everything."

"OK," said Visalam, her reluctance visible in every part of her, in every movement of her every limb.

"Good evening, Doctor. This is my friend Visalam from the office. She hasn't claimed a single medical bill."

"Hmm. What amount do you require?"

"16,000."

"Shouldn't really be a problem. We will show two days in the hospital and a small surgery. The balance can be for medicine. I will include the usual commission."

Visalam had been quiet all the while, just paying whatever Lata told her to and giving whatever detail the doctor wanted. On the way back to the house, she went to the temple and prayed. She sat in the temple for a long time, thinking over what she had done and then walked back to the house, her feet dragging at every step.

When she reached home, she put the false bill in front of the image of the Lord and said, "I don't know what else I can do. I hope I have done the right thing."

She bathed and changed and went to bed that night without cooking or eating.

When she submitted the bill at the office the next day, she was surprised at how easily the entire matter proceeded. "Haven't seen any of your bills before. Everything OK?" She nodded and went back to her own office. She collected the cheque from the office, which she deposited in her bank.

She called Vibhuti in the evening. Even before she could say anything, "*Perimma*," she shouted, I know you have got it! Right?" The lilt in her voice shook Visalam. How could she ever have thought of not getting what Vibhuti so dearly wanted?

***

Vibhuti had tears in her eyes as she recalled the incident and all that followed. "At that time, I did not really know *perimma*'s financial state. All I knew was that here was one source from which everything I ever wanted always came. I had no idea of what she was going through."

Sridhar's usual cheerfulness was very subdued. "When Vibhuti gave me the racquet, I was simply overwhelmed. I had not really expected it. Between my sister Sudha and Vibhuti, they managed to convince the Yonex distributor that it was for me. They had taken all the documents to show my State ranking. Only later, when I quizzed them both, did I come to know who had arranged the money," Sridhar added. "At that time, my focus was on improving my ranking in the State and getting a good national ranking. And with the help of my new racquet and–as I realized later–with the blessings of Visalam *perimma* and Vibhuti's love, I did make good progress."

"Ya Allah. This is amazing," said Ali

***

On her next trip to Hyderabad, Vibhuti hugged her aunt and couldn't thank her enough. "I have always maintained you are the bestest, *perimma*." she kept repeating.

Sudha and she took Visalam to the Academy where Sridhar was playing. Indeed Visalam could see a marked freshness in his game. He seemed surer of himself and his ability. "What a remarkable change a racquet seems to make!" Visalam wondered.

But what gave her solace and enormous happiness was the change in Vibhuti. She seemed like the old Vibhuti, full of life and pleased with herself. She was once again calling everyone her 'best friend', though Sudha remained on top of her list of friends.

After his game, Sridhar came over to where the three were sitting. "*Perimma* (Sudha and he had also taken to calling her *perimma*), Vibhuti told me that you were instrumental in getting the racquet for me. I really don't know how to thank you. This has been such a boon for my game. I am sure on current form I will make it to the national ranking next year. The racquet seems to operate as an extension of myself and seems to know exactly what I am trying to do the shuttle. It is just fantastic."

In private, Visalam contemplated on what she had done. Had she done something that was outside her *dharma*? Could her action be justified in any way–to the world and, more importantly, to herself? Is the fact that doing what she did seemed to be the 'social norm' within her company give her the right and the freedom to do it?

Does the pleasure of seeing the happiness on Vibhuti, the very joy of her life, and removing the despondency in the child's face, outweigh the moral latitude she had given herself?

She had no answers, but when she was with Vibhuti and saw her happy, nothing else seemed to matter so much.

Visalam got back to the routine of her work and her prayers. While she could never get over the uncomfortable feeling of having done something that transgressed her own moral norms, life got along pretty well. She was recognized for her work in the office; Vibhuti called regularly and sounded very happy, talking incessantly of Sridhar and his progress on the court.

"*Perimma*, tomorrow is a big match for Sridhar. He is pitted against the number 1 in the state. He has been working very hard and is confident he will be able to beat him. Pray for his success. I will call you tomorrow and tell you what happened."

Visalam had always included Vibhuti's health and happiness as part of her daily prayers. Lately, thanks to Vibhuti's constant reminder to pray for Sridhar, she had included his success also.

"Guess what? Sridhar has just been ranked State No.1!!!!!!! You should have seen him play yesterday. I was reminded of what you told me about his powers of concentration. Once the game started, I don't think he knew anything else, like Arjuna. He beat the No. 1 (now former No.1!) quite easily. The way Sridhar smashed, his opponent could do nothing. And when he smashed, Sridhar was ready and made some fantastic returns. I tell you, *Perimma*, Sridhar will be National No.1 before long. And all thanks to you. You are the best."

Visalam looked for the newspaper in the office to see if the story was reported, but did not find a mention. However, Vibhuti sent her a cutting from the local paper.

"This young boy, Sridhar," wrote the sports correspondent, "has the potential to be a world beater. He has the height, the skills, and economy of movement on court to be able to return almost anything thrown at him. His coach agrees that the one area he may need to do more work on is the backhand flick from the baseline. However, he has shown enormous capacity to work hard and to learn. Today, he is the top ranked player in the State, in a State that is bursting with highly talented youngsters.

It won't be long before we see him on the international stage."

Every time she spoke to Vibhuti, Visalam felt good and the burden she was carrying of having got false medical bills slowly began to fade.

Unfortunately, there was an international clean up in Qubec Technologies and several frauds were detected, among them people claiming money on false medical bills. In the Indian office of Qubec, over 70 people were asked to leave on grounds of lack of integrity. It made headline news across the country. Some of the senior people were also asked to leave and others posted in their places from different parts of the world. Many of the managers who came out clean were sent to other country operations; often to replace managers who had been asked to leave. Based on the auditor's report, several systems changes, among them the system of claiming medical expenses. The company made internal audit systems stronger and more frequent.

An audit team from the Head Office, headed by a Canadian, spent over a week in Indian office of Qubec (as they did in other country locations) to ensure that the systems were fool-proof. Among the many major decisions, one was to ask all their major suppliers to submit to audit by the same international auditor. The directive from the Head Office was that the company across the globe should not only be clean themselves, but should associate only with suppliers who are also as clean.

Visalam's company was a Tier-I supplier to Qubec Technologies. There was panic as many realized that they too might get in the firing line. There was urgent scrambling as people tried to straighten their personal records. Accounts Department worked overtime trying to make the documents and records up-to-date and accurate.

The auditors arrived at the company, sending panic waves among all the employees. They were given the use of a vacant office and all records made available to them. They worked diligently for several days, and had several meetings with the top management of the company. They also called most of the employees for one-on-one discussions on specific details. When Visalam was called by the auditors, she was on tenterhooks.

"Yes. This is a false bill," said Visalam when confronted with her medical bill. "I never had this disease nor did I spend this money on hospitals or medicines." Visalam was calm, dispassionate and pale. She had spent several hours in the last few days thinking about what might happen and begged forgiveness of Bhagawan. She knew in her heart that if she were asked about the false bill, she would not be able to tell a lie.

"What did you tell them?" asked Lata when Visalam came out of from the meeting with the auditors.

"The truth."

"You should have denied it completely. The doctor who gave us the bill would back us."

"Is that what you are going to do?"

"Yes. The fact that you told them it was a false bill is a bit scary."

"What do you think they are doing?" asked a young technician. A few of them were at the lunch table, along with a colleague from the Accounts Department.

"These people seem very thorough. They have already asked some very uncomfortable questions about our accounting practices. However, it appears that their mandate is not to discredit the company, but to ensure that the systems we have are fool-proof. Thank God, we have done no funny business in our dealings with them or with any of the Government Departments. I believe some of the other supplier companies may be in trouble. I overheard them talking to each other."

"What do you think will happen to us?"

"It appears that they have taken greater cognizance of the more recent falsehoods. They are spending more time on bills, invoices and other documents pertaining to the last couple of years."

At the end of audit, there was a recommendation from the Qubec that a list of people provided by the auditor be given notice for various types of irregularities. Among them was also Visalam's name.

Visalam's boss called her to his office. "I am really sorry, Visalam. You are one of the best people in this office--in terms of work, as well as a person. I have fought hard with our MD as well as with the Principals. Unfortunately, the Principals are unwilling to make any changes to the recommendation made by the auditors. It seems so unfair. The phone rang. "Yes," he barked into the phone. "No, please hold all calls for a while."

"However, I have insisted on two concessions in your case," he continued, "One that you will not be sacked, but allowed to resign on your own. Second, knowing your level of integrity, I have also got him to agree that you will give one-month notice, which will be accepted by the company. Others are being asked to leave immediately. I am really sorry. It is the best I could do. The way I have worked it out, your leaving will at least not be directly linked to this mess. I will also happily give you a strong recommendation to wherever you apply."

"Thank you, Sir. I really appreciate what you have done for me. It is more than I deserve."

***

Vibhuti's tears continued to flow. "I came to know of her sacrifice only later. At that time, she did not tell anyone about what happened. She never let on that she had to cross her own moral and ethical boundaries just to see me happy. I must have done something really good sometime to deserve the love of someone like *perimma*."

"What happened to her friend, Lata?"

"That is the interesting part. I found out later that Lata was not among those sacked. She and many others had been doing for years what *perimma* did very reluctantly, just once. Many of them, including Lata, escaped. I really don't know how."

"What happened to her later?"

***

CHAPTER VII

Visalam submitted her resignation, citing personal problems for wanting to quit (that she argued with herself was, in fact, the truth). She tried her best to focus on work and act as normally as possible. The others named in the auditor's report had been given marching orders the very next day.

There was a sombre air in the office. Many who knew they had been guilty of the same crime as that for which others had been sacked were either sheepish or aggressive or somehow feeling they were plain lucky.

The talk around the lunch table naturally revolved round the same subject.

"I am not sure what criteria they used to identify those who they thought were guilty on various grounds."

"Someone in Accounts told me that they really looked at depth over transactions in the last year or two."

"We have been somewhat lucky," added the accounts officer, "Some other companies have been pulled up severely for bad accounting practices and loopholes in their processes. I know of at least one company that has been removed from their supplier list."

"I really feel sorry for Ramanan. He is absolutely shattered. And with a disabled daughter at home, he is in great trouble."

"I believe some people have actually committed suicide in their own offices in South East Asia Region of Qubec."

Visalam simply heard them, but made no comments of her own. She seemed to have gone into herself.

"What a relief," said Lata a few days later to Visalam, "we both escaped!"

"No. I have been asked to leave. I was on that list."

"What? How can they do that?"

"Only GM has taken my side; he fought with the MD and got him to agree that I will resign on my own for personal reasons and that I would be relieved after the usual notice period."

"I am so sorry, Visalam. Why would they pick on you? You are the straightest person I know–may be even more than necessary!"

"Somehow I knew the day I agreed to give in false bills that things would go wrong. However, I can't even begin to tell you how wonderful it felt to see Vibhuti happy. She had been very upset over the previous several days. Just to see her so happy is almost worth trouble. I just can't see that divine girl unhappy."

"All the same I am really upset that you have been named in the list."

"Don't worry too much. I will get another job and GM has promised to help."

"Have you already submitted your resignation? When are you to be relieved?"

"Yes. Two weeks from now. I have asked for a one-week leave from next week. I have a lot of leave accumulated and GM has allowed me to encash them."

Visalam spent four days of her one-week leave at and Ashram with Swami Atmananda. She was not ready to face Vibhuti, lest she let slip words that will tell her of what she was going through. She told her sister that she was quitting because of office politics, without giving any details. Lakshmi had agreed with her that spending time with Swamiji is perhaps the best.

Visalam had come to the Ashram two days ago and spent her time listening to Swamiji's talks and attending *puja* at the temple. She had asked Swamiji for some time to talk about what was happening to her.

"Swamiji, why is it that two people doing the same kind of action, right or wrong, suffer differently?" she wept.

Visalam narrated the whole sequence of events to Swamiji, including her apprehensions and hesitations, her not being able to see Vibhuti unhappy, her helplessness, her capitulation, the consequence, her being asked to leave. "The only positive aspect has been the response of my GM. I have been working with him for almost 3 years now and he apparently fought with our MD as well as with the principals. While they could not stop my name being on the list of people to be terminated, he managed to convince them that I should be treated as a separate case and be allowed to resign rather than be terminated. He has tried his best to ensure that my leaving cannot be connected to the events in the office. I learnt later that he, in fact, put his own position at risk fighting for me."

"In this world, many things are not what they appear to be."

"Most people in the office give in false medical bills and claim. In fact, this has more or less been the norm. I did not agree and did not ever claim against a false bill. It was the combination of my desperation and Lata's argument that everyone does it, so it is almost part of the salary package that pushed me into doing it. And for quite some time, I suffered internally for it."

"You are a sensitive person and have a strong conscience with clear moral values. You have offered prayers to the Lord and asked for forgiveness. The fact that you are suffering as a result of what you did is also part of the *prayaschitta phala*, atonement."

"Only when I saw Vibhuti so happy was I able to convince myself and not suffer too much internally."

"She is certainly a wonderful child. And you have taught her many good things. Even at her young age, I am sure if she knew you were doing things for her happiness against your moral values, she would have told you not to do it."

"That is why I am so thankful that my GM has kept me away from being branded a cheat–at least formally. All the same, Swamiji, why is it that so many others who also have done what I have–in fact, many of them do it regularly–don't get punished, while I do."

"Isvara. God, Bhagwan is everywhere in the form of order. One such order–in fact, a key one–is the law of karma. It never fails. Karma as defined in our scriptures is action done by a human being wilfully."

"Only humans?"

"Yes. It is important to understand this. Animals do not have karma. They are programmed to do whatever they do. Karma follows a *jiva*, the individual across all births. What one goes through today is not only a result of what one has done in this lifetime, but across many lives."

"Have you ever wondered why one person is born to material wealth, while another to very poor parents? Why one person is born in a family of erudite scholars while another is born in a family where no one has had any education? Why one person in the same family is born of fair skin, while a sibling is dark skinned? Or, among sisters one grows up lean while another has a tendency to put on weight even when on a strictly controlled diet?"

"Yes, Swamiji. In my school there were a couple of us friends who used to talk about this. We debated if this could not be totally random, but never really got an answer."

"It is not random at all. It is all part of the order of *Karma*. Where and what circumstances one is born is dictated by the actions of the *jiva* in previous births. That is the only logical explanation that covers all the known facts."

"Swamiji, Dr. Ravichandran from Chicago is on the line," interrupted a *brahmachari* who was taking care of Swamiji's affairs.

When he had finished the conversation on the phone, another disciple of Swamiji, a Brazilian named Sofia came to do *pranams* to him.

"Om," said Swamiji, "We were talking about *karma*. You can also stay."

"It is easy to accept that the things we have no control over–where we are born, to what parentage, what siblings, in what circumstances etc.–are results of our *karma*. If one can extend the same logic to whatever happens to one in life and accept that that too is also a result of some *karma*; *karma* done either in this lifetime or in previous lifetimes."

"Yes, that is easy to understand." Sofia.

"However, it is sometimes not so easy to relate to this in one's life. Since every *karma* has *phala*, fruit–seen or unseen, every *phala* in the form of the situation that we find ourselves in must also have some *karma* as the cause behind it. When did the person do that *karma*? Unfortunately, we with our logic and reasoning, can only infer that it must have been done sometime before the *phala* resulted; we can rarely say, when, where and what type of *karma*. But the law of *karma* is invariable and inevitable."

Visalam said, "That would also explain why sometimes an apparently good person is burdened with extreme sadness. We had a neighbour; a very good man, very religious, very giving, upright whose son died in a car accident in Bombay. His son was 27 and doing very well. The father has been shattered ever since."

"The fact that we cannot see the cause and effect together makes it very difficult for most humans to relate to this immediately. However, a little thought would make it clear that if one is put into a situation that is unpleasant or undesirable, it is the result of something done earlier."

"I have a doubt," said Sofia, "The fact that we find ourselves in unpleasant situations is a result our own previous actions. However, does the law of *karma* only result in out being placed in an undesirable situation or does it mean that we have to actually suffer in order for the *karma phala* to exhaust itself? What I am saying is that one could, say, be insulted by someone on the road out of road rage. That is unpleasant. But one could also not give it any importance and therefore not suffer much because of it. Does that mean that another unpleasant situation will come along till the person actually exhausts the *karma* by suffering?"

"That is an interesting question," added Visalam. "I have also sometimes thought about this."

"It is indeed an interesting question. The result of one's *karma* is only to put one in situations that are pleasurable or unpleasant, depending upon the *karma*. Whether one suffers due to an unpleasant situation depends on the individual. Clearly, the greater the maturity one has to deal with unpleasant situations, the less will he or she suffer for it."

"How do we use this knowledge in practical terms? I know I have not really done much wrong, certainly much less than many others around me, who have done worse things and more often. Yet, I get into situations of discomfort while many of them don't."

"The understanding of the infallibility of the law of *karma* should immediately put any comparisons out of the equation. And yet, the internal disturbance has to be put to rest. If one could actually do something about any situation, one would never feel depressed or frustrated. It is the helplessness of the person in that situation that leads to many problems. In normal course, when we get into situations like that and we are unable to do anything, what does one do?"

"Seek help from someone else?" Sofia.

"Right. Look around and see if you can find someone who has more knowledge about the subject and/or more power to do something in that area. As a child, one went to one's parents or to the teacher when one found oneself in such a situation. They always helped make it better, because we believed they had more power and/or knowledge. Extend this to *Isvara*, the Lord, when in trouble of any kind. The very act of praying gives you something to do about your situation. You will no more be in a state of helplessness, and therefore rid yourself of the resultant depression, frustration etc."

"Thank you Swamiji."

Sofia and Visalam prostrated before him and left.

As they were walking out, Sofia said, "I read a very interesting book. Many well-known people have endorsed it. In fact, they have actually said that they practiced what the book talks about and that it works.

The primary point it makes is that when anyone appeals to the Universe with intensity and a sure belief that it will be answered, it is. The book says the Universe responds to appeals made to it. This is nothing but praying to *Isvara* in the form of order, like Swamiji says. Another point the book makes it is that the appeal should be positive. For example, instead of praying 'I should not fail in this examination', one should pray 'I should pass with flying colours'. The theory being that the universe only responds to the words, not to the content. This is opposite to what we have been taught–that it is the content of the prayer and its depth that makes a difference."

"I have not heard of this book." Visalam.

"I know you are a prayerful person. I am sure whatever situation you get put in, you will not be badly affected or suffer, thanks to your upbringing and your continued prayers."

Visalam returned to the office, feeling a lot better. As soon as Lata saw her, she exclaimed, "Hey you look rejuvenated. More like the old Visalam. The break has certainly done you good."

"Yes, when I have been in the presence of Swamiji, I feel as if all my burdens have been lifted, and there are no problems in life."

On her last day at work, the colleagues gave her a send-off party. This too distanced her from the others who had been asked to leave on the recommendation of the audit team. At the farewell party, all her colleagues spoke highly of her, of her pleasant ways, of her willingness to help her colleagues whenever required, of her personal integrity, and of her efficiency at work. When her turn came to speak, she broke down and could not say anything beyond thanking all her colleagues, especially her boss.

"I am sorry, but it feels as if I am leaving home and I can't stop my tears."

When she went to see her boss before leaving, he got her a cup of coffee and said, "I have spoken to a few people about you for a possible job. There are not too many in our small town. However, please send your resume to these two companies immediately. In both, you can put me down as a reference."

On her way back from work, she went to the temple, walking along the narrow streets, with shops on both sides. At the temple she left her footwear outside, bought some flowers from one of the many sellers of flowers and other puja material outside the temple. She went in, gave the flowers to the temple priest who recited mantras and put the flowers at the feet of the idol. He then showed camphor light to the deity, in an act called *aarti*. He then took out a small part of the flowers and gave it to her with some *vibhuti* and *kumkumam*. She accepted them with devotion, applied the *vibhuti* on her forehead. After her prayers and walking around the sanctum sanctorum–clockwise–she sat in the outer compound of the temple, contemplating on her current situation and on her future. Was she in the current state of uncertainty because she had done something wrong? Or, was she considering her action as being wrong on hindsight, because of where she was now?

Suppose Row Fine Parts had not been forced into the kind of audit with Qubec, would that have been the best result? Who or what decides these circumstances? Is that what we call God?

Any number of things could have happened–Qubec need not have gone into overdrive with their global audit on company frauds; Or, if they had not found too many major problems in the Indian operations and therefore not taken it further to their suppliers in India; Or, if they had, they could have applied different criteria for picking who should be asked to be relieved of their duties. For example, if they had considered the number of medical claims over the last few years and taken for close examination only those that had exceeded a certain number, she might not have appeared on their former list.

Visalam contemplated. "It is obvious that there are many factors over which I did not have any control at all. In fact, there were many factors I could not even have thought of. How on earth could I have imagined the string of events that did take place, and that brought me to this current situation?

Of course, I had a choice. I remember Swamiji saying only human beings have a choice. Animals live a programmed life. I can appreciate that. I could have done what I did; I need not have done it; or I could have done it differently. That is the extent of the choice I could have exercised. Who is to say that if I had exercised one of the other two choices, things would have worked out better? What if God were to be waiting for each of us make a choice and then decide what kinds of events should follow so that our prescribed *karma phalas* unfold as they were meant to.

Did my choosing to do what I did influence the other events? Suppose I had not done it, would the rest of the events have taken place the same way? Would Qubec Technologies have done what they did? Or would the course of events have taken a different path? I know what I did was not as per my *dharma*. Did that fact have a bearing on the other events, eventually leading to my being in this situation?

"It is easy to review after the event. But how can one foresee what would happen as a result of what one does, or does not do?"

She decided that she did what she had to do in the given situation and if the consequences were not to her liking, she had to accept them and make the best of them. Her need to see Vibhuti happy had overriding priority. With that thought, she went home, washed and changed, lit the lamp at the altar, said her daily prayers, ate a little food and went to sleep.

She had told Lakshmi and Vasu that she was quitting the job because things had gone stale in the office and, many people had started playing politics. She was not sure how convinced Vasu and Lakshmi were with her story, but she stuck to it. Both of them had tried to persuade Visalam not to give up her job without another in hand. When she was insistent about leaving the company, they tried to persuade her to move to Hyderabad.

"If you are going to quit without another job in hand, why don't you come and stay with us. I am sure there is a better chance of your getting another job here than in our small town."

Visalam was tempted, particularly since it would mean she would be close to Vibhuti, but something held her back from accepting Lakshmi's offer. She was not sure she wanted to be constantly with people close to her, at least for some time.

"Let me see. I have applied in a couple of places. Let us wait to see what happens and then decide," she said.

She wrote to the two companies that her GM had asked her to write to and sent them her resume. While waiting for their response, she used her time listening to Swamiji's talks on various Upanishads and the Bhagwad Gita, worked on her Sanskrit language skills, and read many of the original texts written by Adi Sankara. She continued her usual work routine at home, including taking up of the cleaning of parts of the house that she had been unable to take up for some time.

After a couple of weeks, she got a call for an interview from one of the two companies she had applied to. On the day of the interview, she got ready, went to the temple on the way to the interview and arrived there 5 minutes before the appointed time.

She was asked to wait for a little while. She had found out that this was a small start-up company, doing off-shore work for a major client in the US. It was a neatly maintained fairly modern office, but with strong touches of Indian traditions. There were many scenic pictures of visually beautiful sights, both from the US and India. She recognized one or two of the pictures of Himalayan peaks. There was also a picture of Lord Krishna giving Gita *upadesha* to Arjuna in the battlefield. There were some ethnic Indian curios in the reception area. She felt the office had warmth, unlike some of the big offices where it is all glass and steel and very modern, but impersonal.

The position was that of Secretary to the GM, Mr Kartikeyan.

"Please come in," when she knocked on the door. The GM's office again gave her a sense of ease, with an outer office for the Secretary. The office was not large, but looked pleasant. Mr. Kartikeyan rose from his chair courteously and offered her a chair. He was an elderly gentleman, dressed simply, with a *kumkum* mark on his forehead.

As they talked, he asked her pointed questions about her skill sets and her background.

"You worked in the last company for quite a few years. Why did you leave?"

"The truth is that it was because of the magnanimity of the company and the GM that I left. Otherwise I would have been asked to go, like many others."

Visalam was honest and said it with a straight face.

"What happened?"

"I claimed a false medical bill, there was an audit, and I was asked about it. I told them the truth. They decided to ask me to leave. As I said, thanks to the grace of the top management of the company, I was not sacked but allowed to resign. My justification, if there is such a thing, is that I was informally given to understand that a medical claim up to a limited amount was part of the package, and that most employees claimed it almost as it were part of their salary."

"If that is so, everyone should have been dismissed."

Visalam told the complete story of what happened and how. Mr. Kartikeyan than said, "I am glad you told me the truth. In fact, I had got all the facts from your previous boss, whom I know very well. He also said that your moral and ethical values were impeccable. I think he is right. If you had hidden something of what happened, or tried to be smart about circumventing it, I would have been hard pressed to make you an offer. We are trying to build an honest culture in the company and would like to be very careful about selecting the right people."

"Thank you, Sir."

"We are a small start-up company. My nephew who returned from the US a few years ago set up this company recently. He roped me from semi-retirement to help him in the initial years get the India operation going. He himself spends most of the time travelling, mainly to the US. We cannot match the salary of your previous company, but promise happy working conditions. If you are willing to accept the offer, you will be working directly with me. I think we can get along well. I am happy with what I have seen of you and your previous GM gives you good reference for your work skills."

Visalam was happy to accept the offer. She joined the company soon after. She called Lakshmi the next day.

"Guess what. I have a new job."

"Fantastic! Which company?"

"It is a start-up, promoted by a young engineer from IIT who went to America for further studies, and stayed on. The India end is looked after by his uncle, Mr. Kartikeyan. He is really nice. He was the one who interviewed me."

"When do you join?"

"Next week. I could have joined almost immediately. But I need some time to see Swamiji and get his blessings before I join."

"Wow, great. Vasu will also be pleased."

"Is Vibhuti there? I want to speak to her."

"I will give her the phone. Vibhuti, your *perimma* wants to talk to you."

"Hi, *perimma*."

"I am going to join a new job."

"Wow. Congrats. Will this new job allow you to travel to Hyderabad regularly?"

"I will try and come and see you as often as I can."

"Next time you are here, you will give us a treat, no?"

"Of course. What would you like?"

"I will tell you when you come here. OK. I have to go, My tuition teacher is here. Bye."

"Bye."

She went to Swamiji to apprise him of the developments.

"I got another job, Swamiji!"

"Very good. I knew you would."

"It is a small company, but very good. The GM with whom I will be working is a very nice person."

After taking Swamiji's blessings, Visalam met Sophia.

"Hullo. How are you? Did you read the book I told you about?"

"Yes, very interesting. As I see it, what they call Universe is nothing but God in the form of a universal order."

"Yes, Swamiji often talks of the wrong notions people have about *Isvara*. They think of Him sitting in some place– Heaven or Vaikunta or wherever. God is not a physical form, despite the many, many representations that Indians have. God really is the totality of all beings, *samashti*, in the form of order–physiological order, psychological order, chemical order etc. So, when the book talks of the Universe responding to one's intense desire, expressed clearly and intently, it is nothing but God responding to one's prayers."

"Absolutely!"

"When one hears Swamiji, everything becomes clear. He is a Master."

"And we the lucky ones to be learning from him!"

Visalam joined work the following Monday. Mr Kartikeyan personally took her around and introduced her to the others. She found most of the people warm in their welcome. Within a few days of working, she found that the culture was quite different from what she had seen in the previous company. Mr Kartikeyan and his nephew,

Mr Rajan had established a good set of unwritten rules that everyone seemed to live by. Salaries and perks were clearly spelt out. Generally, no one made any attempt to cheat the system. Their dealings with vendors, employees, and anyone else interacting with them were polite, clear, unambiguous and straight forward.

Visalam blended in very easily and was soon accepted by everyone. When Mr Kartikeyan learnt that she was a disciple of Swami Atmananda, he was impressed. He had high regard and reverence for Swamiji, although he himself did not visit him often. He supported some of the projects of Swamiji, especially those relating to education for the underprivileged. He donated significant amounts of money, both from his personal accounts as well as from the company.

Mr Rajan visited the India office about 6 months after Visalam had joined the company. He spent about two hours with her and his uncle, talking about the values he wanted to establish in the company. "Today we are small. It is easy to ensure that values are maintained. As we grow bigger, get more people on board, open more offices, it will become more difficult to see that everyone follows the same culture. It is therefore, very important that we make it part of the basic, unchanging culture of the company right from the very beginning."

On his request, she approached Swamiji to come and talk to the employees. He readily agreed to speak on Leadership. Swamiji explained that every adult was a leader, a *Shreshta*. There are always people who try to emulate one. As a father or mother, they are certainly role models for the children. As a leader, one assumes a responsibility. For people in the corporate world, this role becomes even more important, because inevitably there are juniors who look up to their seniors, watch what they do and then try to emulate them.

When a new person joins a company, he looks around to see what others are doing. If he finds the existing employees (each one of who is a leader in his/her own right) fudging bills, that then is what he will also follow. If he finds that the ones who spend most time in the boss's cabin get the most favours, that is what he will follow. That is how a company's culture is set – by the way people conduct themselves, starting from the top.

Quoting verses from the Bhagawad Gita, Swamiji said that others do what the leaders do. Setting their own personal values and ethics, sticking with them under all conditions is a significant factor in being a true leader. It is easy to be swayed away from these norms by saying "I am doing it for the company." as a justification.

Swamiji left a deep impression on the employees.

One day a technician from another department came to Visalam at lunch. "Akka, I would like to speak to you on a personal matter."

"Sure. At lunch?"

Akka, this life is not worth living," she started to cry. "I don't want to live any longer."

The two of them were sitting in a quiet corner. After she quietened a little, the story came out little by little.

"This is the third party that has come to see me for a possible marriage and rejected me. What is wrong with me?" she said.

"There is nothing wrong with you. The right time and the right man just have not come by. Wait."

According to our astrologer, there is something wrong with my horoscope. That is why my marriage is not getting fixed. Poor Appa is shattered. Already his family is cursing me for being the cause of my mother's death. I feel so unwanted."

"Do you have your horoscope with you?"

"I will bring it tomorrow."

The next day Visalam studied her horoscope and suggested that they see a well-known astrologer she knew at the temple, who could suggest some *parihara*, some mitigating action.

"One is born in a specific situation based on one's past karma. Similarly, one's nature, predisposition, physical and psychological characteristics are also part of what is called *prarabdha karma*. As are the various situations that unfold in one's life. Against this, the wilful actions one does reflect the efforts of will. The best of these is prayer. That is one action that can neutralize, at least partially, the effects of one's *prarabdha karma*. Take your case. You are now in this very difficult situation because of some of your *karma*. Now, how you react is your will. The common feeling in this situation is helplessness. One may look for a shortcut to get out of it by considering suicide. But that is not a good option. There is a better option. Find out how you can minimize the effects. We will do precisely that on Saturday, when we go and see the astrologer and seek his advice for *parihara* actions."

Come Saturday, they went to the temple and consulted the astrologer. After studying her horoscope, he said, "Come here next week. We will organize a *puja* to Goddess

Devi. After that, visit a Sani temple every Saturday and feed at least 2 poor people for the next 9 weeks."

She followed the advice religiously.

She became less depressed, more able to deal with the situation at home and was more effective at work.

Some three months after her visit to the astrologer with Visalam, she came to Visalam and said shyly, "My marriage has been fixed!" One of her distant relatives had seen her at the temple every Saturday, liked her and approached her father for a possible alliance for her son. Things moved quickly from there and a marriage had now been finalized in three months.

"I don't know how to thank you, Akka. The day I came to talk to you, I had made up my mind to end my life. I was unable to see any way out. To me, you are almost God-like! You must come and bless my marriage."

This was not an isolated case of people in the company approaching her for advice and counsel. She seemed to exert a calming influence over people who were disturbed.

It was not long before Visalam had become a sort of agony aunt, counsellor, advisor and mentor rolled into one for many of the employees. She was willing to give anyone time, but insisted that they do it either at lunch or after office hours.

Mr. Kartikeyan was aware of this growing stature of Visalam and was happy that she was there for the employees. He was sure she would be a great positive influence on all of them and a major factor in the establishment of a value based culture in the company.

That fateful day was like any other in her life. She followed her routine, went to the temple on the way to the office and was cheerfully focusing on her work. She was concentrating on some papers that she was dealing with, when she suddenly crashed on her table, knocking down her keyboard.

"Saar," the peon ran into Mr Kartikeyan's room, "Visalam Akka has fainted."

Kartikeyan immediately arranged for an ambulance. He called up a doctor friend, a senior consultant in the hospital. He also drove down the hospital to meet with his doctor friend.

"It is nothing serious. However, during the examination, we noticed a lump in her breast. It may be nothing, but it is better to get it checked," said the doctor.

"Are you thinking what I am?" Kartikeyan.

"Hopefully it is nothing. But, as I said, it is better to check it out."

Kartikeyan arranged for Visalam to have mammography done at the same hospital. The results were inconclusive.

"I am OK, Sir." Visalam said to Kartikeyan. I don't think we need to worry any further."

Mr Kartikeyan, however, was unconvinced. Ever since his friend the consultant had spoken to him, he had been seriously concerned. Although his friend did not specifically say anything, Kartikeyan sensed that he suspected that it could be serious.

He insisted on further tests. He spoke to his friend and asked what else could be done to make sure it was nothing.

"Let us do a needle biopsy, and if necessary, follow it up with a core-biopsy."

As it happened, the tests were still inconclusive, but left a trace of suspicion. Overruling Visalam's objections, he sent her to Chennai to a major hospital to get a thorough investigation done, praying that it would confirm the benign nature of the lump.

Unfortunately, the Lumpectomy only confirmed the presence of cancerous cells in her body – invasive ductal carcinoma stage 3-b.

Kartikeyan asked hundreds of questions of the doctors. Whether the cancer could be controlled at this stage, what was the treatment etc. She was often very tired.

Visalam took a few days off to go to Hyderabad to be with her sister and her darling niece. Vasu took one look at her and said, "Akka, is everything OK? You are looking really pulled down."

"Nothing, just tired. That is why I have taken a few days off work."

Later that evening, when she was alone with Lakshmi and Vasu, she told them about the tests and what they had confirmed.

"There is a very good hospital here, with some of the world's best oncologists. Why don't we take a second opinion?" asked Vasu.

Lakshmi was devastated. "I know breast cancer is common. But how can it happen to you? I can't believe it. I think we should do as Vasu suggests and take another opinion," she said crying.

"I don't think it will change anything."

When Vibhuti heard about it, she did not understand what was happening. She quizzed Visalam about death, about what happens after a person dies, about whether she could still communicate with the person. She wouldn't leave Visalam's side even for a moment till it was time for her to leave. As Visalam was leaving the house to go the station, she hugged her and cried uncontrollably.

When she came back from Hyderabad, she went through a series of chemotherapy and radiotherapy treatments. Either Vasu or Lakshmi (many times with Vibhuti) would come down to be with Visalam every time she had to go for treatment. Kartikeyan also made sure someone from the office would be with her during these times. Every employee was more than happy to be with Visalam and assist her.

She started feeling nauseous often, and her tiredness and fatigue got more frequent. Kartikeyan gave Visalam an assistant to work with. He also gave her a lot of freedom in terms of office timings, and leave -- both to go for treatment as well as for times when she was unable to attend work due to pain or recovery. Kartikeyan instructed his accounts department to cover all bills relating to her illness through a group insurance they had in the office. Both Kartikeyan and Rajan agreed that the company would pay all her medical bills not covered by the insurance. They ensured the best medical care.

It was becoming more and more difficult for Visalam to get to work. The company allowed her unlimited paid leave.

"Sir, I think I would have to move into the hospice soon. Lakshmi and Vasu have spoken to a very good one in Hyderabad. I really think that is the best."

Visalam had been on paid leave for several months now, coming into the office only occasionally. The company management and all the employees had been very supportive. Visalam spent a fair amount of time with her sister in Hyderabad. She loved to watch Vibhuti and see how she had grown into a calm, intelligent girl.

"You will, of course, continue to be on our rolls. Your salary will, as usual, be credited into your bank account," said Kartikeyan.

CHAPTER VIII

Visalam entered the hospice along with Lakshmi, Vasu and Vibhuti with a sense of uncertainty. They had visited the hospice a couple of weeks earlier to meet the Director and one of the trustees who had been introduced by Vasu's friend. Visalam found them very sensitive and clear thinking.

"The purpose of our existence is to help terminally ill patients through their last stages. We try and make the last days easy, reduce the pain, not just by medication, but also by actually sharing the pain with them. We pay great attention to helping close relatives deal with the situation."

He had taken them round the hospice and introduced them both to the staff as well as to some of the patients. They were very impressed with the sense of caring that seemed to pervade the entire place.

It was a very well maintained hospice, with the patient rooms around a large water body. Every room had a view of the clean water body with small fountains. Most rooms also had a view of the large garden and hillside. All the rooms were air-conditioned.

The hospice was built on a large land of several acres. It provided some beautiful landscapes, a small wooded area; several gazebos where people could sit, watch nature go by and contemplate.

The rooms were well appointed with a comfortable bed, and another bed for one more person to sleep in. The bathroom was spacious, and clean.

They met many of the patients, and their close relatives. Despite the place being so close to death, there was surprising serenity about the place.

The Director explained, "Late Dame Cicely Saunders, founder of the hospice movement, said to terminal patients, "You matter to the last moment of your life, and we will do all we can not only to help you die peacefully, but to live until you die." That indeed is the principle we also work on."

"Our patients come from all strata of society, from the very rich to the economically challenged. We make no distinction. Indeed, Lord Yama makes no distinction. We do not charge any fees at all. All our services–the rooms, the food, nursing care, medicines, everything is free. The hospice runs entirely on donations. Many close relatives of the richer patients actually come back here and make large donations, either a large one time or sometimes, on a regular basis. Rotary Clubs are among our biggest donors."

"As you have seen we have patients who come from many different parts of the country, and from different religions. This is one place that unites all religions."

Visalam had indeed seen people from various religions in the hospice. There were also arrangements for various religious prayers.

Visalam moved into the hospice about 2 weeks later. Laskhmi took leave from her office and decided to stay with her sister and take care of her as long as was necessary.

Visalam and Lakshmi were in the open area, having a cup of tea, when Nimmi from the next room joined them. She had been looking after her husband, Lalit for over two and a half years now. He was in the final stages. The discussion naturally turned to how one can deal with a situation like the one they were in.

"In Indian mythology, when Parikshit knew he had only seven days to live, he went and met Suka Muni (a *rishi*, a seer), told him about his plight, and asked him how he should spend those days. "You are lucky," said Suka, "You know you have seven days to live. Most of us don't even know if we have one day!"

Visalam said, "Death is a certainty. Any life that is 'born' has to go. It is what is called *anitya* in Sanskrit. There is no permanence. The only reality that is not *anitya* is God. When one gets put into a situation like the one we are in, one should look at the 'now', the 'today'. There is nothing to worry about the future and, the past in any case, cannot be changed. In our situation, there isn't even any lesson that needs to be learnt from the past that can be used in the future!"

"And how should I conduct myself? I feel so helpless!"

"You are doing a wonderful job. You are cheerful, and try to keep Lalit cheerful. You take good care of him and never let him feel that he is alone in his last days. Of course, it helps that Lalit himself has an objective view of life.

That you feel helpless is not such a bad thing. When that happens, we automatically turn to a higher power. Pray.

Let your attitude be prayerful, both for Lalit as well as for yourself. For Lalit, the prayer would probably be to lessen his pain and let the end be smooth, since it is inevitable. For you, the prayer has to be for strength to look after him, to bear and share his pain and, then to deal with his loss when the day comes. One is likely to have a complaint about being a victim–both on Lalit's behalf and on your own–a sense of looking around to see who could be blamed for this current situation. That is a futile exercise and will only lead to more misery. Instead, a prayerful attitude will bring calmness and the strength to deal with the situation without getting perturbed too much. Remember, Lalit needs your support more now than ever before. Only your strength will see you both through these difficult times."

***

Within a few weeks of Visalam's being in the hospice, it had become common practice for many of them to sit around with Visalam and try to catch a few moments of living. Many of them–both the cancer sufferers and the people with them–found great solace in these sessions.

"Everything that happens to us in life must have a cause, isn't that correct?" asked Lalit as he and others chatted with Visalam, "What can be cause of what we are having to go through?"

Lalit was 35 and had been doing very well in life. Though he had a difficult childhood as the family was split when he was just 11, he had shown a cheerful disposition in everything he did. He had graduated in commerce from one of the best colleges in the country and gone on to do his

Master's degree from the London School of Economics. He had been working in a large Consulting company in India and was transferred to the International Head Quarters in London. He was respected in the company as much for his knowledge and ability to get things done, as for his cheerfulness and, for pursuing his goal relentlessly.

He had married Nimmi, also a graduate from LSE, 8 years ago. For the first 4 or 5 years they had a wonderful life – everything that a young couple can dream of. Each was intensely in love with the other and, between them, had material success, respect at work and in society. However, about three years ago, he had been diagnosed with blood cancer. Neither gave up on life and continued to live their life to the full, even as they went through all the treatment that modern medicine could offer. His pain level kept going up, but the level of joy they exhibited in each other and in life, never diminished.

Lalit now was in his last days and they had come to the hospice through a friend. Nimmi insisted on staying with him all the time, looking after all his needs. She knew that he would not last much longer and that she would have to bring order to her own life. However, she did not want to think about it. Earlier today, Lalit was in great pain and the nurse had just given him a shot of pain killer.

"True," said Visalam, "Every result must have a cause and every action must have a result. This is our common experience and everyone intuitively or, through reasoning and logic, understands this. It is clear that every experience we undergo is a result of a cause. Sometimes we are placed in pleasant circumstance that seems to evoke a sense of pleasure or joy. Other times we end up in unpleasant situations when we tend to ask 'why me?' In either case, the cause has to be in what one had done sometime earlier. Sometimes we can easily identify the effect with the cause, but more often than not, especially in situations like these, we cannot see the connection very easily."

"When you say unpleasant situations, you mean like illness or pain?" asked Mariamma Kutty, once of the nurses in the Hospice.

"Yes, but also pain caused by emotional hurt, and intellectual suffering. Pleasant and unpleasant experiences come and go in everybody's life, one after the other. When we get into pleasant situations, the tendency is to attribute it to our own efforts that we can recognise. 'I did such and such, and am reaping the benefits'. Many people who have achieved successes in their own field of endeavour and have been recognised by others, tend to attribute the success to hard work etc. Some people say 'it is God's grace' without actually meaning or understanding what they are saying. However, in almost all cases, everyone knows deep in their own hearts that there are many more factors–contributions of many others, of 'luck', that ephemeral factor that no one can put a finger on–that have placed them there, even if they do not acknowledge it to everyone."

Sekhar, who was looking after his mother in the hospice, said, "Most of us tend to blame other people or events for our unpleasant experiences. Someone sent me a nice one from the net the other day, which says that most people would say, 'I got here on time' when they are on time and 'Wretched traffic. Got delayed so long at that stretch of road', when they are late."

"True. When we get into difficult situations, such as the ones we are all in, very few people can accept that it is the result of something they themselves may have done."

David, another cancer patient whom the doctors had given up on some time ago, but was still around, asked, "You mentioned that we are often not able to connect the cause and effect. Why is that?"

"There are two reasons. Firstly, we often do not remember things we did in this lifetime, leave alone what we may have done prior to it. Secondly, for every action, there are two types of results – those that we can perceive immediately as a result of an action and relate to the action, called *drishta*, and those that we cannot see, called *adrishta*. As a simple example, *drishta* result of doing regular physical exercises would include both better health as well as the sense of well-being. Or, when one reaches out to help another person, with no ulterior motive, one gets a sense of satisfaction as a *drishta* result, but we know intuitively that there is bound to be another aspect of result which we may not be able to relate to the act itself. When and how that result comes about is not possible to predict."

"True," said Sekhar, "A friend of mine used to say that we somehow 'know' that a good act will result in something nice happening to one. However, if one does an unselfish act for the benefit of another, it is not as if that the recipient of the 'good-act' will return the favour to the same person sooner or later. Every act – good or bad – actually goes round, may be round the world, but comes back to one in some form, at some time, through someone. That makes a lot of sense to me."

"That still does not take away from the fact that each person here is suffering, whether he is a patient or is nursing a loved one," said Mariamma Kutty. She had seen enough of the physical pain that the patients go through and the emotional pain that the relatives go through waiting for the end, and later, trying to cope with it.

"A wise man once said, 'Suffering is voluntary!' Life offers us many situations, good and not-so-good. The undesirable situations can be in terms of physical pain, or worse, emotional pain. One really has little or no control over this.

However, how one responds to a given situation is something that is will-based and one can control to a large extent. People with the same illness often behave is entirely different ways. One person may, for example, moan and complain, while another may not take much notice of it and go about whatever is to be done normally, so much so that others don't even realise that the person is in pain, and yet others may simply take alleviating medicine and try and get over the pain. What is the difference? It is not in the pain level or in the type of illness. It is to do with the individual – one may think of it in terms of ability to bear pain or better, in terms of maturity."

Nimmi chipped in, "Reminds me of my grandmother. No matter how much pain she was in, there was no change in the household routine. I believe many people, particularly women of that generation, had that capacity."

Such sessions with Visalam had become common in the hospice. Almost every day, there were deaths and the fear of imminent death was palpable. Most of the people there found some solace in these discussions and Visalam's objective view of the world and of life.

***

"I used to visit *perimma* as often as I could. The hospice was surprisingly warm for a place that had human death written all over it. Some of the staff told me that Visalam's serene presence had actually made the entire place more cheerful.

I was also present in many of these discussions. She seemed to somehow induce a sense of 'all-is-well' and 'whatever-happens-is-to-the-good' in everyone around. There was one Mirza Ghulam there, who told me that he used wait for these sessions. He was there with his wife, also a terminal breast cancer patient. He would then go back to the room and tell his wife everything he had heard. He told me that his wife was actually able to face death a lot more easily after these discussions. In fact, after his wife died, he stayed on in Hyderabad for some more time, just to be able to participate in the discussions. I was told by someone at the hospice that he made a large donation to the hospice.

Perimma was certainly a great influence on everyone in the hospice, including the staff. Everyone noticed Visalam being cheerful amidst the tragic surroundings. Where most of the people were sombre or serious, she would, despite the pain, meet the others cheerfully and give them comfort."

***

The staff at the hospice found in her a wonderful human being who could actually reduce others' pain by simply sharing it with them. They themselves were very sensitive and caring, but willy-nilly, over time, they did get hardened to human suffering and, to death. Every once in a while, they did come across someone who would not be cowed down by the surroundings or his/her own suffering.

Visalam's presence was a great blessing to everyone in the hospice, both the patients as well as the people looking after them. It was almost as if by her very presence she was able to boost the positive energy in the system. She never seemed to be overly burdened by her own situation.

When Nimmi and Lalit were alone in the room, she said, "Sometimes I feel like a withering plant that has been thirsting for water. Just being with her is like getting a dose of refreshing water, leaving me able to smile."

"Yes, I know. My pain also seems to be much more manageable. And I am able to appreciate your beauty even more!" Nimmi blushed a pretty pink.

"Nimmi, you are still a very beautiful woman. I am so lucky to have someone like you around and gain your love. Your last few years have been a total loss, looking after me."

"Not a waste at all. Especially after the understanding that Visalam has given us. I think it my very enjoyable duty to be with you at this time."

"Nimmi, I want you to promise me that you will get on with life in the next phase and not act the traditional Indian wife and mourn for your husband forever!"

"I don't want to think that far. We are together and I want to savour every moment of this togetherness."

Lalit died the next day, as peacefully as is possible in such circumstances. Lalit's parents as well as Nimmi's parents came down for the funeral. They also did the entire rituals that are prescribed for the 13 days. Nimmi was a vision of strength and calmness during the entire time. She shed a quiet tear, but for the most part, she dealt with issues effectively, meeting relatives and friends squarely, accepting their condolences calmly.

It was only after some time, when she was alone with Visalam that she broke down and cried her heart out.

"Despite all that you have taught me, I can't help feeling I didn't deserve this."

"It is OK to cry," said Visalam. "We play several roles in our lives and each role calls for different feelings and emotions. You have been a fantastic model for everyone. You have shown maturity beyond your years."

As Nimmi calmed down, Visalam suggests they move outdoors, closer to nature. They pulled up a couple of chairs to the edge of the water body in the hospice. There was a gentle, caressing breeze blowing that seemed to carry some of the pain away.

"Ah, beautiful! Amidst such natural beauty, no one can be down for long." exclaimed Visalam.

"I know. But, it feels as if there is nothing left for me. I love him so much. He was everything to me. I am not even sure how I am going to manage my life from here on. Unfortunately, my parents have not been of great help. Right now, I feel so alone."

Visalam said, "What you have gone through–and are going through–is tough. You have shown great character in dealing with it. Lalit will perhaps continue to be part of you for ever, irrespective of what happens,"

"I am wondering if I should dedicate myself to the study of our scriptures, under Swamiji. He has given me so much in the last several months."

"No. Try and get back to as close to your normal life as possible. Live your life fully. Taste the world; understand its values as well as limitations. When the time is right, you will turn to serious study of Vedanta, I am sure. For the immediate present, get back to your life, to your work, to your parents, friends and relatives. This is indeed the time you will also discover who really cares for you and who gets close to you with an agenda. You are young, good looking, and intelligent, with a good job .... and perhaps vulnerable. Don't get into a long-term relationship for some time. Absorb the loss of a part of you in terms of your relationship with Lalit. Continue to pray for him to attain *moksha*, if not immediately, then for him to be born in circumstances that are comfortable and conducive for the pursuit of the truth."

***

Visalam became well-known for helping people with emotional problems. A leading newspaper did a story on the Hospice. The reporter was so impressed with how Visalam was being a source of enormous strength not only to the patients and their close relatives, but also to the staff at the hospice. The fact that her own life had been full of problems and that she was herself in enormous pain never seemed to come in the way of her being of help to others.

The story on the hospice that was carried in the newspaper as a full page feature said:

> We were amazed by the work being done at the hospice–the care and sensitivity being shown, the compassion of the care-givers, including the maintenance and cleaning staff. The whole hospice is being kept so clean and spic-and-span that one could be in one of the better 5-star hotels anywhere in the world. And all this without charging any money for any of the services.
>
> Among the patients and their loved ones, we found a lady, Visalam, who seemed to be in the centre of things and yet, was unobtrusive. She shied away from speaking to us about herself. However, every one we spoke to at the hospice had such amazing stories to tell that we would not be faulted for thinking she is a saint–maybe she is. Our crew also felt the power of her presence in the few short hours we spent at the hospice.
>
> "Human society finds it very difficult to deal with death. Even though everyone knows that he or she must die someday, the imminence of death seems to make it very difficult for one to deal with it. It is also extremely difficult to watch someone you love writhe in agony, knowing he/she is doomed to great pain till death provided an end to it. The symptoms of the terminally ill can be physical,

emotional, or psycho-social in nature. We try to bring comfort, self-respect, and a sense of peace to people in the final stages of life. Our attempt is to control the patients' pain, and support their emotional needs. We believe that the end of life should not be a medical experience, but a human one, an experience that should not be in a clinical hospital, but in surroundings that are home-like and pleasant. That is one of the reasons we have such a large area that allows the patients to be with nature as much as possible," says Mr Reddy, a trustee of the hospice and a prominent businessman of Hyderabad.

When asked about the phenomenon called Visalam, he said, "She has been a terrific supplement to all that we have been trying to do for our patients. She provides such support to the patients and their relatives that it lightens up the whole place. Our endeavour has been to create an atmosphere where death does not hang as a heavy issue, despite the fact that there is a death almost every day. She truly contributes in this. Also, her ability to absorb physical pain and the ability to face death have induced great confidence in everyone, including the staff at the Hospice."

We know there are several *mahapurshas* in the world. But to have the fortune to stand along with one of them is a blessing and honour I and my team of journalists and photographers will cherish.

***

Her sheer presence seemed to help heal many a hurt. Several people come to see her, just sit, hear her talk to others, and return to their homes feeling a lot lighter and less disturbed. It became common for people who were not even in the hospice to come to sit in at these discussions. It started with some of the relatives of the patients and their care-givers, but grew rapidly to include many others.

During these sessions, people spoke to her about their own problems, or about the many aspects of life itself. Some people asked specific questions which she would answer. She also talked about common problems generally.

"How do I manage my anger?"

"Anger – and indeed many other emotions – is not voluntary. If you were told to get angry now, it would be very difficult to do so. Try it. The only issue is that one's anger should not victimize anyone else. This implies that one does not immediately express one's anger as far as possible. One should process such emotions. Such emotions are also part of the order of *Isvara*. Accept anger also for what it is. Take an example of a person driving in heavy traffic. At the traffic lights, when the light turns green, he finds another motorcyclist cutting across all the way from the extreme lane to make a U-turn. He brakes hard. Nothing happens, other than the fact that the motorcyclist merrily goes his way. It is a situation strong enough to make him angry. How does he deal with it? He could also make a wild U-turn, chase the motorcyclist with the intention of accosting him. Or he could shout the choicest abuses at the person. Or he could mutter under his breath about 'these brainless motorcyclists who are a menace to society'. In all these cases, he makes himself susceptible to bad driving. On the other hand, he could do what one of my friends said he does in such situations – make up a story about how the motorcyclist is rushing to the hospital to see his son, who has been admitted in the emergency ward, or that he is going to see his already upset girl-friend and is running late. With that he calms down and continues his car journey without getting unduly disturbed.

Anger typically is a desire that has been frustrated. The problem with desires is that it can never be satisfied. If it is satisfied temporarily, desire for more of the same arises before long. Sooner or later, desire remains unfulfilled and leads to one of the negative emotions, anger, frustration, depression etc."

***

"The old gentleman in room 7, Mr Roberts, died last night."

"Poor thing. He suffered so much. I understand he was a Brigadier in the army. But I must say his children were marvellous. They looked after him in turns. Visalam Ma'm helped the relatives deal with it, giving them courage and strength."

Such conversation was common at the hospice. Almost every day, someone or the other would breathe his or her last. It had become an accepted practice for the relatives to call Visalam whenever a patient died, irrespective of the religion, economic status, and whether many close relatives were present or not. It began to be believed that if Visalam was there at the death or immediately thereafter, the soul of the person would not suffer.

One day, Sekhar came to see Visalam and said, "Amma passed away a little while ago. Will you come and bless her?"

Visalam went with Sekhar, despite her own considerable pain. Sekhar's wife, his brother and his sister-in-law had also reached there. As she entered the room, the sense of gloom seemed to lift a little. Sekhar's wife, who had attended several of the informal sessions at the hospice, touched her feet. Her sister-in-law followed suit. She comforted them, blessed them and after a few minutes, left for her own room where Lakshmi (who knew that Visalam was in great pain herself) was waiting with the nurse. The nurse gave her a strong dose of pain-killer by injection. Visalam was soon asleep.

***

"By the time it was clear that her own end was near. Her pain had become quite severe, although she never showed it. It had also begun to occur more often and for longer periods. My mother was with her constantly. I had started to spend as much time as I could with *perimma*. I saw at close quarters how she seemed to give courage to people. Many of the patients and their relatives started to come to see her in the room and talk to her.

This was about the time you guys came into her sphere of influence. Obviously, there was some connection between all of us that circumstances brought us together, with *perimma* acting as the cohesive force."

"It is interesting that you should say that, Vibhuti," said Mark. I was reading a book by a famous psychiatrist the other day, where he tries to establish that we all come across the same set of people in different lives, in different forms. Despite the fact that I was brought up to not accept that we have many lives, I found it fascinating to read. May be we are connected not only in this life time, but from before."

Ali said, "With all my religious learning, I think impossible having this conversation with people like you. It clear whatever happening cannot be result of my experiences in this life. There is special bonding between us. Why we drift to each other even middle of so many people? What drawed me to each one of you, I don't know. But something did. Lady Visalam, of course, uniting, pull all together. But, there were so many other people, including my own countrymen, but this bonding not happen.

***

Visalam died quietly one day. She looked as calm in death as she did before. At that time, Lakshmi, Vasu, Vibhuti and Sridhar were with her. She knew her time was over. She called each one individually to her bedside, held his/her hand, looked into the eyes, and in her own quiet way blessed each one of them.

Mr. Karthikeyan had been to visit her two days before on one of regular trips to Hyderabad. He had kept in close touch with the hospice. He came back as soon as he heard the news. Mr. Rajan was in the US and regularly spoke to the hospice and to Visalam on the phone. He could not make it to be with the family for the last rites.

When the news of her death spread, everyone in the hospice came to her room to pay their respects–patients and the relative/s with them, irrespective of when they had moved into the hospice, every member of the staff from the housekeeper to the Director, and most trustees came to see her. No one shed a tear, despite the loss many felt. She seemed to be among them encouraging each one to respect life, of which death is only a part.

Mark, Adrian, and Ali remained with Vibhuti, her parents and Sridhar all the time, helping in any way they could. Each seemed to be in total contemplation with himself, but made sure he was available to Vibhuti and Sridhar whenever required.

CHAPTER IX

Several months later

"This has been one of the most exciting matches I have ever seen!" The commentator, herself a former champion could hardly contain herself, "The last point, stretching to a 27-shot rally must rank among the best ever – especially on the last point in a crucial final."

"Both players have shown incredible athleticism, picking up and returning shots that looked almost impossible," added her co-commentator.

"Right through the tournament, they have both exhibited a standard way above what one had come to expect of them. The younger Singaporean has been showing tremendous promise right through the year, but this has clearly been his best."

"Both Sridhar and Wong have beaten higher ranked players on their way to the final. Both looked unstoppable. It is unfortunate that only one can win. Both deserved to win."

"I will relive the last point in my mind several times over. Starting with the short service by Wong, both showed total all-court craft of a very high order. Sridhar's cross-court smash somewhere in the middle of the rally looked like a clear winner. How Wong returned it and then continued to fight will make for wonderful repeated viewing. Front-back-side-to-side, both running the other, but neither ever letting up. Amazing. Let us catch the post-match interview."

Interviewer: What a match! How do you feel?

Wong: Exhausted; on top of the world.

Interviewer: Did you feel at any point in the match that you will win?

Wong: No. It could have been anybody's match. Sridhar played a fantastic game. Hats off to you, Sridhar.

Interviewer: You repeatedly raised your game a notch each time Sridhar looked like getting a grip on the match. What drove you?

Wong: True. Every time I thought I had taken control, Sridhar just lifted his game. Fortunately, I too was able to raise my game at crucial points. Thank God. I am not sure I will ever be able to produce the same again.

Interviewer: I am going to ask Sridhar to join us. Sridhar, would you call this your best match ever?

Sridhar: Undoubtedly. This has been the best result for me. I tried my best. But Wong was there every time I thought I had won a point. He somehow managed to return the shuttle. Not just return, but put it in a place in the court that did not allow me to take advantage of my previous shot. The last rally was one that

I will–and I am sure Wong will–remember for a long time.

Interviewer: Both of you reached the final the hard way–eliminating higher ranked players along the way in some really tough games. Did the fact that the number one seed had to pull out because of injury affect how you went about it?

Wong: No. I would have fought as hard. I am sure I speak for Sridhar as well.

Vibhuti could hardly contain herself. As soon as possible, she ran on to the court and clung to Sridhar, interminable tears streaming down her cheeks. "I wish *perimma* was here to see this. We owe her everything." This was her refrain every time Sridhar achieved something in the world of badminton. He rose rapidly in the National rankings and remained in the top five. Vibhuti tried to go to every match Sridhar played in the country, even if she could not do so when he was travelling outside for tournaments. And every time he did well, she clung to him, tears streaming down her face and said, "I wish *perimma* was here to see this. We owe her everything."

This was the first major international tournament outside India that she had been able to go to. And what a tournament it had been!

Back in India, Sridhar was feted by the sports community, with congratulatory messages pouring in from various quarters, including political leaders. The State Government allotted him an apartment and awarded him a cash prize. When they did get a quiet moment, Sridhar and Vibhuti decided to have a private dinner at home.

"Visalam *perimma* has been such a factor in my life. But I constantly feel the pain of her suffering. I have had to reason with myself and, thanks again to her, I have realized that no one ever achieves anything on his or her own. No one can claim to be a self-made man. There are always many others, without whom that success would not have been possible. It is true. I have looked at many examples. One group, for example, that stands out is school teachers. Most of them never see any material success. It is also true that but for their support, many would not have reached the peaks in their field that they did. I will take you to meet someone very special tomorrow to prove my point."

Vibhuti perked up, "Who? Please tell me."

"Wait till tomorrow. You will see."

Next morning.

"Are you ready?"

"Ready? I have hardly slept, wondering who this very special person is."

"Let's go."

Driving through small by-lanes, Sridhar took her to a small house in a narrow street. "What kind of very special person would live here?"

Sridhar smiled and knocked on the door. After a longish gap, there was some shuffling and an elderly lady opened the door.

"Who," she said, squinting through narrowed eyes.

"It is me, Sridhar, teacher," said, Sridhar, bending down to touch her feet in a mark of respect.

"Oh. I remember you. Please come in."

They entered a small room, with two plastic chairs and an old television, covered in lace cloth. Though small, with very few things, it was kept neatly. The walls had several photographs, many of them old class pictures.

"Teacher, this is my friend, Vibhuti. This is Jaya teacher. She taught me maths in school." Vibhuti touched her feet.

"I learnt only recently that you had come to Hyderabad. I wanted to share my joy. I just returned from Singapore, having won the Silver Medal at an international tournament."

Her eyes seemed to suddenly light up with joy.

"How wonderful! Which sport?"

"Badminton."

They stayed for about 10 minutes, while she cajoled them into having coffee and biscuits.

On the way back, Sridhar said, "She was one of the earliest people to shape me into what I am today. One may argue that teaching mathematics has nothing to do with success in badminton. But I do believe every bit goes towards making one what one is."

"I know what you mean. For every Sachin Tendulkar, there are several contributors, not forgetting his early coach, Achrekar."

"Precisely. I now view Visalam *perimma* also in the same vein. She held out her hand so I (and you) may step on it and climb higher. Whatever we were able to do for her later will never be any match to what she did."

"True. But I can tell you that every time she heard about your success, her whole demeanour would brighten. Just like Jaya teacher's when she heard of your Silver Medal," said Vibhuti with an impish smile.

"Visalam *perimma* taught me to appreciate that one is inextricably connected with everyone else, and that one is the totality of everyone put together. That understanding allows one to be humble and grateful. It is not only the obviously visible sacrifices made by others that have made one what he/she is. Sure, to the visible one can and should pay ones tribute, but understand that there are many other "sacrifices" that have been made by many others. That is why mentally I dedicate every medal I win to all of them (of course, with *perimma* and you on top of the list!) Without this clarity, I would be so guilt-ridden that I would never have been able to play to my potential. Hey, I got a congratulatory message from Clara and Mark also."

"Hey, isn't it wonderful news about Clara? She sounded so excited! She said if it is a boy, she is going to name him Krishna."

"In fact, both Mark and Clara seem to be so happy. The other day Mark spoke to me and he sounded so happy with the world. Not that they don't have problems. He spoke to me about some of the problems as well. But, they have found a beautiful way of supporting each other that no problem seems too difficult to handle."

"I like Mark. He is truly in love with her. He will do anything to keep her happy."

"Clara spoke to me about their differences in religion as well. But they seem to have found a way of allowing the other enough space to be. Mark is especially sweet. He goes to the temple with Clara sometimes, even though he says he still cannot relate to it. Clara told me Mark continues to go church, but is beginning to find happiness in the temples as well."

"Did she talk about what happens when the baby begins to grow? Which religion will he or she follow?"

"They have talked about it at length. They intend to expose the child to both–Church on Sundays and Temple on Thursdays! And then allow the child to choose at the right time. I am sure they will handle it right. They have *perimma*'s blessings. Mark told me that religion is about as close to one's being as anything can be. He was so certain that he could never give up the Church. It was an integral part of him. If he were to give up his religion so as to get married to Clara, a part of him – a significant part of him – would be lost forever. However, after seeing *perimma* and hearing her story, he realised what she had given up was far more critical than religion. And she suffered as a result. But, in that suffering she grew many times in stature. He felt much more comfortable in accepting that Clara could be together for life, even if she follows a religion that he does not understand or believe in at all."

"Mark was only doing what many people do with their religion–using it as a support in their quest for something that life and known science is not able to give answers to. Mark is objective enough to realise that. However, he told me he has no intention of giving up being a good Christian. He will continue to follow his religion, but with much greater understanding, maturity and acceptance of other forms of living."

"Sad we couldn't go for their wedding. I believe both Adrian and Ali managed to go for the wedding. It would have been nice to have met everyone. Hopefully we will meet all of them at Adrian and Julia's wedding."

ALI

Ali left Hyderabad and his new-found friends, feeling a lot better with himself. He was still not sure how he was going to handle the situation. He was sure that whatever steps he takes (including not doing anything) will lead to difficulties, but felt confident of handling it.

Soon after returning home, he made preparations to visit his step-sister in the hills, where he was sure Asghar had gone. He took a bus to Abra, the nearest town, and stayed the night in a small hotel. Early morning, he washed, bought some naan and some fruits and set out on foot for the farm.

His prayer beads never stopped clicking. There was not even a road in the remote place, only a small footpath. He followed the path, climbing over several small hillocks. He continued to pray. Each time he sat down to eat or to rest, he would think about Visalam and his new friends. Ali wondered how each was handling his/her life. They had parted company after those wonderful two days, when they shared each other's stories and found an unearthly connection between all of them. "Each of us lived such completely different lives and yet found something common, something touching each one of us," he thought to himself, not for the first time. "I wonder what draws us together."

After two days of trekking, he finally sighted the hill on which his half-sister's farm was located. The path all the way had been dry and the sun unforgiving. There was little shade. There were hardly any human beings along the way. He encountered only a few stray animals. However, he found a few small settlements, many of them temporary. At each he was warmly welcomed, allowed to rest his feet, given food and water, and at night a place to sleep. He thanked them, but did not disclose where he was headed. Nor did they show much curiosity. Such is the nature of living in the wilderness.

Ali started the final part of the journey, trekking up this last hill slowly and arrived at the farm near dusk. He was tired and dirty. The first person he saw was Asghar, looking defiant, confused and scared at the same time.

"Baba!" he exclaimed, "How did you come here?"

"I know you very well, my son," said Ali embracing his son, with tears in his eyes.

Ali sat down to rest his tired legs, as Salma walked in from the farm.

"Ali!" she exclaimed, "I knew sooner or later you will come here looking for Asghar. You must be tired. Come and have a wash, while I get some hot food ready for you."

Later in the evening, Ali asked Asghar, "Where is your friend?"

"I don't know. But when he saw someone coming up the path, he ran away. I am not sure where he has gone."

"Do you know that the police are looking for your friend? And you also?"

Asghar looked even more scared than he was before. "Sharief and others inducted me to help them. I am scared. I don't want to be with them. The days I spent here with Sharief have not been good."

They sat through most of the night, talking. Ali persuaded Asghar to come back home. He assured him that the Imam would see that no harm came to him.

The next day they took leave of Salma and started back. Asghar continued to be fearful of what would happen. Ali was also unsure of what might happen when they got back home, but was hoping that he would be able to talk to the Imam and ensure that nothing unpleasant happened to Asghar.

They reached Abra after a couple of days of trekking and decided to stay there for a day. There they heard that Sharief had been captured and was being deported to America for questioning. Ali had to truly become the father that he once was and held Asghar close to him, repeatedly reassuring him. It was clear that Asghar had got into a situation beyond his control. "Baba, I am afraid. I lied to you and forgot all the lessons on love that you taught me. I am scared of being in jail."

After they reached home, Ali left Asghar at home and went to see the Imam to tell him what had happened. He told him that he had found out where Asghar had gone and brought him back with him. He also told him that Asghar seemed to have got into wrong company, but was repentant.

The Imam asked him to bring Asghar to him. He spent quite some time with him, alone. When Asghar returned, he was still apprehensive.

Despite the Imam's efforts, Asghar was arrested and tried for abetting a terrorist. However, he was not given the kind of treatment generally meted out to such people. A proper court heard the case and sentenced him to seven years in prison.

Ali was shattered. He knew he had no choice and that either way, he would have to suffer. That knowledge, however, did not make it any easier for him to deal with the situation. The Imam used all his power and influence to see that Asghar was treated well and that Ali could visit him regularly.

"What I am going to do? How am I going to manage my life now? By the time Asghar comes out of jail, I will be a broken man." he lamented to the Imam.

"Have courage. He has to pay for his mistake. I have ensured that he is treated well. I know of a group that works across the world, the members of which work to help victims of terrorist attacks. It would do you good to work with them. I will speak to them and arrange for you to meet them."

"Thank you. I would like that very much."

Ali went through several rounds of interviews with members of Love Without Limit, LWL, an NGO headquartered in Geneva. "Our aim is two-fold. First, reduce the pain of being an innocent victim and of suffering losses. Second, reduce possible hatred for those who caused it and not carry a sense of revenge. That is the way the vicious cycle of hate and destruction can be minimised. We are happy to see that you too think along the same lines and are pleased to induct you as one of our volunteers. We are very careful to see that all those who work with us are people who genuinely want to see hatred reduced. Welcome to what we believe is the most important mission in today's world. Welcome aboard LWL."

Ali threw himself wholeheartedly in the work relating to LWL. Initially he worked in the office for several months. Following that, he was part of a team that went to many other countries where terrorist attacks had left a scar on people. He would return to visit Asghar at regular intervals and tell him many stories of what he had seen and heard. Asghar was truly repentant of what he had been involved in in the brief, misguided period of his life. He was proud of what his father was doing and swore he would join him as soon as he finished his sentence.

Ali seemed to have found a new purpose to life and he was delighted to see the new Asghar.

ADRIAN

He knew his life can never be the same again. He planned to talk to Julia and then ask Rose for a divorce. Knowing Rose, he was prepared to lose all his wealth. That, however, did not bother him. He was sure he would make a new life for himself with Julia, even if he had to start from scratch. He knew he would have a tough time on his return. Only he did not foresee how tough.

***

"Let's get married, darling," said Rose, "I want to be the mother of your, no, our children. I want to be able to stand up and say, I am married to the most wonderful man on earth."

"We have discussed this before. I would love to. But how do you get rid of Adrian? He will not agree to a divorce."

Rose was in Florida with Roger, Adrian's boss. They had been having a roaring affair for over two months. Rose had found out that Roger was independently rich and owned significant shares in the company as well. She also knew he was a recent widower with no children.

She had met him a couple of times at office get-togethers and had her eyes on him. She felt she had got everything she can from Adrian. She knew she could go much higher. Her opportunity came once when Adrian had to go out of town urgently and miss an office party. Rose asked if she could get someone single from the company to escort her to the party. Adrian had agreed. She went to the party with Roger. She danced with many, but most intimately with Roger. She knew many young girls in the office were also eyeing him. She pretended to be not-easy-to-get, but would send invite signals to him every now and then.

When Roger dropped her back, she invited him in for coffee. One thing led to the other, and Roger spent the night with her. He was smitten.

"Hook, line and sinker!" she said to herself and made herself unavailable to Roger for the next couple of weeks. He did call her several times, but each time she made up excuses. She knew she had him. Gradually, she allowed him inside her circle and held on to him. The next problem was to find a way to marriage. The stumbling block was Adrian. How could she make Adrian agree to a divorce?

She had given it considerable thought. She was in Roger's house the time Adrian was away in India. "Roger, sack Adrian. The job market is not good. He will not find another job easily. Let me see if I can work around getting him to agree to a divorce."

"Good idea. We are in the process of downsizing. I will make sure Adrian's name is on the layoff list."

When Adrian returned, he had a nasty surprise waiting for him. Roger was all sympathy, but pretended to be helpless.

Rose's reaction when he told her about it was explosive. "You are a fool. I have been telling you forever to be more assertive at work. You will never amount to anything. How are you going to support the family now? I am not willing to lower my living standard."

Julia's reaction was very different. "Oh, poor Adrian! I am sure you will find another job quite easily. Sometimes I do not understand the basis on which a company lets go of people. It appears to me that they let go of some of the better people. One of my managers once told me that downsizing often hits the very efficient. His argument was that these people already draw heavy salaries at an early age and would continue to be a huge draw on the company resources. I am not sure how right he was. But certainly, in your case, it seems to me that the company has let go of one of their best."

As days and weeks went by without Adrian being able to secure another suitable job, Rose got shriller about what a waste Adrian was. Adrian was reluctant to go to Julia in the current situation. Julia was sad. She knew what Adrian was going through, but did not understand why he was not sharing with her all that he was going through. At times, she felt that he was avoiding her, hiding himself inside his own cave. Once when she insisted on meeting and sharing his troubles, he was, for the first time in their relationship a little testy. Julia was shocked. Adrian realised he had hurt her, and was instantly remorseful. "I am sorry, sweetheart. It is just that I need time with myself to deal with the situation," Julia could still not understand why he would not want to be open with her. She was sure she would be best support he can get. "That is how men are," said Adrian. "We like to be able to present our best side to our girls, not open all our problems to her."

Adrian knew his bad times will eventually give way to good ones. He had come prepared to deal with the problem of divorce. He did not anticipate problems piling on him like this. He had lost his job, for no fault of his. He knew he was good at what he was doing and that he was contributing to the company. The air at home, indifferent before, had become intolerably tense. Rose made it clear that she thought he was incompetent and useless. He also suspected that she influenced Paul by her attitude. To top it all, he wanted to be with Julia, but not under these circumstances.

Adrian was waiting for an appropriate opportunity to broach the topic of divorce with Rose. He was not sure how he should raise the topic, especially at this time when he was feeling a little below par.

One day, Rose herself gave him a cue. "If you cannot manage a family, why did you get married? And stay married? Get out, get a divorce," she said. Adrian reacted like a cornered cat, just as she was hoping he would. "OK, I will get out; and apply for a divorce."

Rose sensed her opportunity and shrieked, "What do you mean, divorce. Who will look after me, and young Paul? How will we live? If divorce is what you want, divorce is what you will get. But I will take you to the cleaners. I am going to see my lawyer." And she stormed out.

Unknown to anyone, Rose had already talked to her lawyer and had everything ready. The divorce papers were served on Adrian within days. Adrian did not contest and Rose was awarded all the assets he had–the house, the car and all his investments. The judge was lenient enough to not award Rose any part of any future earnings.

All Adrian had was what was in his bank savings account; And a few clothes. Adrian walked out of the house, feeling sad, but greatly relieved. He had been caught in a situation where any action he took (including inaction) would result in hurting someone. Thanks to the sense of objectivity that he gained during the short time he spent with Visalam, he felt this was an acceptable outcome,. Julia met him and took him to her apartment. She tried to be a support to him, without hurting his male ego.

The next few weeks were very difficult, both financially and emotionally. He continued to look out for a suitable job, but it was not easy to come by. He tried his best to keep his spirits up, and help Julia as much as he could.

Till one day, he called Julia at work and said, "Julia, let us go to the theatre and dinner tonight. I have picked up tickets for a nice romantic comedy. I will meet you outside your office."

"Wow. Wonderful. But I need to go home and freshen up and change!"

"No. I have been seeing you every day when you return from work. You look beautiful. We will not have much time. The play starts at 7."

"Wow. You look gorgeous!" said Adrian as he picked her up from outside her office. They enjoyed the play, holding hands. Julia had tears in her eyes. Adrian felt like the man she knew before. She knew the last few weeks had been very tough for him, and indeed, for her.

"That was most enjoyable. Where are we going for dinner?"

"You will see." There was a smile on Adrian's face.

He hailed and taxi and they went to a small boutique restaurant. They were ushered to a table Adrian had already reserved for them. Their table was specially arranged with lots of flowers and a bottle of Veuve Clicquot waiting in an ice-bucket.

"I love you very much. What is the occasion?" asked Julia.

Suddenly, musicians appeared at their table, with soft serenade music. Adrian got down on his knees, as all the staff of the restaurant stood around them and said, "Will you marry me, Julia. Your happiness will be my happiness for the rest of my life." He opened a ring-box and presented her a simple diamond ring.

"Yyyyes." she blurted, blushing furiously.

The entire restaurant stood up to applaud. Julia could feel the red rising to her cheeks like never before. The story came out during the rest of the dinner. All Adrian's efforts at finding a job had been unsuccessful. It appeared to him that there was not even a lower level job available. Out of the blue, he got a call from one of the Headhunting firms, asking to meet. From there it just went rapidly. Before the day was over, he had met the Chairman and President of a relatively new start-up. He had offered Adrian a senior position. The salary was somewhat lower than what he had been drawing, but the company offered him stocks, after an initial period of 6 months. Adrian was delighted and was determined to propose formally to Julia–and make it an evening to remember.

The rest of the evening and night were like a dream for Julia. She was so happy. Even more, she was happy to see Adrian break out of his difficult mould that he had set in over the last several weeks.

The wedding was fixed for six months later. Adrian called up each of his India-found friends and insisted that they come for the wedding and meet Julia. Post the wedding, Adrian had organised a special dinner only for Sridhar and Vibhuti, Ali and his brother, Mark and Clara.

"I am very happy you could all come for the wedding. This is just like the time in Hyderabad, with the added pleasure of my beautiful wife's presence."

"Adrian has been talking so much about all of you. And about the wonderful woman you all met in India--- Visalam. I wish I too had had the opportunity of meeting her. I am really glad all of you could come."

Ali said, "Despite my credentials as member of international organisation that the US agree is doing good work, I had difficult time at immigration. But, I understand their anxiety. I can only pray that all hatred and fear is removed from the minds of all people."

"How is Asghar doing?"

"Very well. He is still in prison, but is well. He has started to teach reading and writing to other prisoners who are not literate. He also looks after their library now. I am hoping that he would be released well before his term. Thank Allah, I have got my Asghar back, even if I can only see him in prison for some more time."

"Excuse me. I have to feed little Krishna." So saying Clara went away.

"Life is a conundrum. Dilemma was there, and will be there. Let us pray that those facing such situations find the source of strength to deal with it."

Amen.

*****

AFTERWORD

Hope you have enjoyed reading the novel. It is all about the situations—situations that we come across quite often in our own lives. Many times, we face a dilemma because our decisions and actions lead to someone getting hurt (even if it is oneself) irrespective of the decision or action we take. The hurt could be physical, emotional or even intellectual. I do hope, dear reader, that you will be able to relate to one or more of these situations, having seen something similar in your own life or in the lives of those close to you.

No living being wants to be hurt, and will take any action that will reduce or eliminate the possibility of getting hurt. Of all living beings, human beings are special—not only do we want not to get hurt, but are also aware that no other being wants to get hurt. This is often the cause of dilemma that one faces, even if one does not recognise it.

The level of internal conflict varies depending upon the individual, his/her sensitivity and the situation. Sometimes we are faced with a sense of guilt (or hurt), and sometimes we put up a stout defence. The defence mechanism is often seen in bluster, in aggressiveness, in a sense of frustration etc., or expressed in words like, "I had no choice", or "Better he is hurt than me".

What you have read is only a few of the possible situations that, hopefully, cover a wide range. Many other situations also lead to similar dilemma. If you would like to share any of your experiences or those of others you know, do write to me at ganesh1948@yahoo.com.